God Lives in St. Petersburg

"The stories in this fresh and skillful collection center on American expats—often sick, dazed or unable to communicate—struggling to make sense of the politicpal and cultural landscape. . . . Memorably sparkling."
                    —*Newsweek International*

"Graham and Ernest move over, you've got company."
                    —*Kirkus* (starred review)

"Marvelous . . . unforgettable. . . . Bissell, young as he is, up-to-the-minute in subject matter and anointed with po-mo glamour . . . is nevertheless a traditional writer, a master of the well-made slice-of-life."
                    —*The New Leader*

"Bissell's stories are long and bursting at the seams with clever dialogue, well-sculpted settings and full characters. It is a rare pleasure to find a young writer handcrafting prose with such patient care. . . . The stories chug to dramatic and emotional peaks, then plunge earthward, leaving the reader shaken and dazzled."
                    —*The Moscow Times*

"In spite of its grim setting, *God Lives in St. Petersburg* is a hoot to read, full of laugh-out-loud turns of phrase. . . . Bissell builds a footbridge between our world and his characters', and does it better than just about any other young writer today."   —*The Hartford Courant*

God Lives in St. Petersburg

TOM BISSELL

Tom Bissell was born in Escanaba, Michigan, in 1974. After graduating from Michigan State University, he taught English in Uzbekistan as a Peace Corps volunteer and then worked for W. W. Norton and Henry Holt as a book editor. He is also the author of *Chasing the Sea*, a travel narrative, and (with Jeff Alexander) *Speak, Commentary*, a collection of fake DVD commentaries. He is a contributing editor for *Harper's Magazine* and *The Virginia Quarterly Review*. His work has appeared in the *Pushcart Prize Anthology*, *Best American Travel Writing*, *Best American Science Writing*, and *Best American Short Stories*. He currently teaches in Bennington College's low-residency MFA program and lives in New York City.

ALSO BY TOM BISSELL

Chasing the Sea:
Lost Among the Ghosts of Empire in Central Asia

Speak, Commentary:
The Big Little Book of Fake DVD Commentaries,
Wherein Well-Known Pundits Make Impassioned Remarks
about Classic Science-Fiction Films
(with Jeff Alexander)

God Lives
in
St. Petersburg

and Other Stories

TOM BISSELL

Vintage Contemporaries
Vintage Books
A Division of Random House, Inc.
New York

For my mother

FIRST VINTAGE CONTEMPORARIES EDITION, JANUARY 2006

Copyright © 2005 by Thomas Carlisle Bissell

The stories in this collection were previously published in the following:
"Aral" in *Agni*; "Expensive Trips Nowhere" in *The Alaska Quarterly Review*;
"Animals in Our Lives" in *Bullfight*; "God Lives in St. Petersburg"
in *McSweeney's* and the *Pushcart Anthology XXIX* (W. W. Norton, 2004); "Death
Defier" in the *Virginia Quarterly Review* and *Best American Short Stories 2005*;
"The Ambassador's Son" in *BOMB* and in the anthology *Wild East: Stories from the
Last Frontier* (Justin Charles & Co., 2003).

Permissions to reprint previously published material can be found at the
end of the book.

The Library of Congress has cataloged the Pantheon edition as follows:
Bissell, Tom, [date]
God lives in St. Petersburg and other stories / Tom Bissell.
p. cm.
1. Americans—Asia, Central—Fiction.
2. Asia, Central—Fiction. I. Title.
PS3602.I78G63   2005
813'.6—dc22   2004052232

Vintage ISBN-10: 1-4000-7542-4
Vintage ISBN-13: 978-1-4000-7542-3

Book design by Pamela G. Parker

www.vintagebooks.com

146614399

The Heart asks Pleasure—first—
And then—Excuse from Pain—
And then—those little Anodynes
That deaden suffering—

—Emily Dickinson

Contents

Death Defier

Graves had been sick for three days when, on the long straight highway between Mazar and Kunduz, a dark blue truck coming toward them shed its rear wheel in a spray of orange-yellow sparks. The wheel, as though excited by its sudden liberty, bounced twice not very high and once very high and hit their windshield with a damp crack. "Christ!" Donk called out from the backseat. The driver, much too late, wrenched on the steering wheel, and they fishtailed and then spun out into the dunes alongside the road. Against one of the higher sandbanks the Corolla slammed to a dusty halt. Sand as soft and pale as flour poured into the partially opened windows. The shattered but still intact windshield sagged like netting. After a moment Donk touched his forehead, his eyebrow bristles as tender as split stitches. Thin watery blood streaked down his fingers.

From the front passenger seat Graves asked if the other three men—Donk, Hassan, the driver—were all right. No one spoke. Graves sighed. "Glad to hear it." He gave his dune-pinned door two small impotent outward pushes, then spent the next few moments staring out the splintery windshield. The air-freshener canister that had been suckered to the windshield lay quietly frothing lilac-scented foam in Graves's lap. The spun-around Corolla now faced Kunduz, the city they had been trying to escape. "I'm glad I'm not a superstitious man," Graves said at last. The driver's hands were still gripped around the steering wheel.

Donk climbed out on the Corolla's open side, cupping his throbbing eye socket and leaning forward, watching his blood patter onto the sand in perfect red globules. He did not have the faintest idea what he had struck his head against until Hassan, wincing and rubbing his shoulder, muscled his way out of the car behind him. Hassan looked at Donk and shrug-smiled, his eyes rimmed with such a fine black line they looked as if they had been Maybellined. His solid belly filled the stretched sack of his maroon cardigan sweater, and his powder-blue *shalwar khameez*—the billowy national pants of Afghanistan, draped front and back with a flap of cloth that resembled an untied apron—were splattered with Donk's blood. The whole effect gave Hassan an emergency-room air. Donk did not return Hassan's smile. The night before, in Kunduz, after having a bite of Spam and stale Brie in the rented compound of an Agence France Presse correspondent, Donk and Graves found their hotel room had been robbed. Graves had lost many personal items, a few hundred dollars, and his laptop, while Donk had parted with virtually all of his photographic equipment, including an irreplaceably good wide-lens he had purchased in London on the way over. Hassan, charged with watching the room while they were out, claimed to have abandoned his sentry duties only once, for five minutes, to go the bathroom. He had been greatly depressed since the robbery. Donk was fairly certain Hassan had robbed them.

Donk fastened around his head the white scarf he had picked up in Kunduz's bazaar. Afghan men tended to wear their scarves atop their heads in vaguely muffin-shaped bundles or around their necks with aviator flair. Afghanistan's troublous Arab guests, on the other hand, were said to tie the scarves around their skulls with baldness-mimicking tightness, the hem just millimeters above their eyes while the scarf's tasseled remainder trailed down their spines. This was called *terrorist style*, and Donk adopted it now. It was the only way he could think to keep blood from his eyes. He also sort of liked how it looked.

"Hassan," Graves snapped, as he climbed out of the Corolla. It was an order, and Graves—a tall thin Brit with an illusionless, razor-burned face—had a voice seemingly engineered to give orders. He had thick brown hair and the ruined teeth of a man who had spent a large amount of time in the unfluoridated parts of the world. His hands were as filthy as the long sleeves of his white thermal underwear top, though his big fingernails seemed as white as shells. Graves made his way to the truck, twenty yards down the road and askew on its three remaining wheels. He glanced down at the tire, innocently at rest in the middle of the highway, that had shattered the Corolla's windshield. Donk noted that Graves looked as stately as was imaginable for a sick man wearing one of those silly war-reporter khaki vests and red Chuck Taylor

All-Stars. Hassan rushed to catch up to him, as Graves had not waited.

This left Donk and the driver, a kind of bear-man miracle with moist brown eyes and a beard it was hard to imagine he had not been born with, to have a look under the Corolla and assess the damage. Monoglots each, they could do little better than exchange artfully inflected grunts. Nothing seemed visibly wrong. The axle, for instance, was not bent, which had been Donk's greatest fear. But the steering wheel refused to budge and the ignition responded to the driver's twist with a click.

"Hmn," Donk consoled him.

"Mmn," the driver agreed.

Donk looked over at Graves, who was speaking through Hassan to the truck's stranded driver. Graves was nodding with exquisitely false patience as the curly-haired boy, who looked no older than twenty, grasped his head with both hands and then waved his arms around at the desert in huge gestures of innocence. Bursts of dune-skimmed sand whistled across the three of them. The bed of the boy's truck was piled ten deep with white bags of internationally donated wheat. His truck, Donk noticed, was not marked with any aid group's peaceable ideogram.

It had been a strange morning, even by Donk's standards. A few hours ago some "nasties," as Graves called them, had appeared on the outskirts of Kunduz, though they were supposed to have been driven out of the area a week ago. In fact, they were supposed to have been surrendering. Graves and Donk had jumped out of bed and rushed downstairs into the still-dark morning autumn air to see what they could see, hopping around barefoot on the frigid concrete. The battle was still far away, the small faint pops of gunfire sounding as dry as firecrackers. It appeared that, after some desultory return fire, Kunduz's commander called in an American air strike. The great birds appeared with vengeful instantaneousness and screamed across the city sky. The sound was terrific, atmosphere-shredding, and then they were gone. The horizon, a few moments later, burped up great dust bulbs. But within the hour the gunfire had moved closer. The well-armed defenders of Kunduz had been scrambling everywhere as Donk and Graves packed up what little remained of their gear into this hastily arranged taxi and sped out of town to the more securely liberated city of Mazar.

"Bloody fool," Graves said now, when he walked back over to Donk. He was speaking of the curly-haired boy.

"Call him a wog if it makes you feel better," Donk said. "I don't mind."

Graves cast a quick look back at the boy, now squatting beside his hobbled truck and chatting with Hassan. "He's stolen that wheat, you know."

"Where was he going?"

"He won't say."

"What's he doing now?"

"He's going to wait here, he says. I told him there were nasties about. Bloody fool." He looked at Donk, his face softened by sudden concern. "How's that eye, then?"

"Bleeding."

Graves leaned into him optometristically, trying to inspect the messy wound through the do-rag. "Nasty," he said finally, pulling away. "How many wars did you say you've covered?"

"Like war wars? Shooting wars? Or just wars?"

Graves nodded. "Shooting wars."

"Not counting this one, three. But I've never been shot at until today." While they were leaving Kunduz their Corolla had been hit with a short burst of Kalashnikov fire, though it was not clear that the bullets were intended for them. The driver had used the strafe—it sounded and felt like a flurry of ball-peen hammer strikes—to establish a median traveling speed of 125 kilometers per hour. They had very nearly plowed over a little boy and his pony just before the city's strangely empty westernmost check-point.

"And how did you find it?" Graves asked, as though genuinely curious.

"I found it like getting shot at."

"That was rather how I found it." Graves's face pinched with fresh discomfort. He sighed, then seemed to go paler. His eyelids were sweaty. Graves stepped toward the Corolla searchingly, arms out, and lowered himself onto the bumper. "Think I need a rest." The driver fetched a straw-covered red blanket from the Corolla and wrapped it around Graves's shoulders.

They had been in Kunduz for two days when Donk noticed Graves tenderly hugging himself no matter the heat thrown off by their hotel room's oil-burning stove. His pallor grayed by the day, and soon he was having trouble seeing. Initially Graves had not been concerned. They went about their business of covering the war, Donk snapping Kunduz's ragtag liberators and the dead-eyed prisoners locked up in one of the city's old granaries, Graves reading ten hours' worth of CNN updates a day on his laptop and worrying over his past, present, and future need to "file." But his fever worsened, and he took a day's bed rest while Donk toured Kunduz on foot with the city's local commander, a happily brutal man who twice tried selling Donk a horse. When Donk returned to the hotel a few minutes before curfew that evening he found Graves twisted up in his vomit-stained sheets, his pillow lying in a sad crumple across the room. "Deborah," Graves had mumbled when Donk stirred him. "Listen. Turn the toaster? Please turn the toaster?"

Donk did not know Graves well. He had met him only ten days ago in Pyanj, Tajikistan, where many of the journalists were dovetailing stories by day and playing poker with worthless Tajik rubles by night. All were waiting for official clearance before venturing into Afghanistan. Graves—with an impatience typical of print journalists, their eyewitness being more perishable—elected to cast a few pearly incentives at the feet of the swinish border guards and asked Donk if he wanted to tag along. Donk, dispatched here by a British newsweekly, was under no real pressure to get in. His mandate was not one of breaking news but chronicling the country's demotic wartime realities. He did not even have a return flight booked. But he agreed.

Donk did not regret following Graves, even as he forced mefloquine hydrochloride tablets into his mouth, crusty with stomach ejecta, and splashed in some canteen water to chase them. Graves, Donk was certain, had malaria, even though it was late November, a season at the outer edge of probability for contracting the disease, and even though he knew Graves had been taking mefloquine since October. The next day Donk convinced one of Kunduz's aid workers—a grim black Belgian—to give him a small cache of chloroquine phosphate pills, as mefloquine was useful mostly as a malaria preventative. The chloroquine seemed to help, and Graves, still as shivery as a foundling, had recommenced with his worries about filing a story. Graves was rather picky with his stories, seeking only narratives that presented this war in its least inspiring light. Unfortunately, Kunduz seemed fairly secure and the people weirdly grateful. Indeed, despite predictions of a long, bloody, province-by-province conflict, 60 percent of the country had fallen to American-led forces in this, the war's fourth week.

After they were robbed, Graves noted that his chloroquine pills were among the missing items. As the regrouped nasties waged this morning's hopeless surprise counterattack, neither Donk nor Graves had the presence of mind to beg more pills before they left, though Donk was fairly certain the aid workers would have pulled out of Kunduz too. That one could simply leave a firefight and come back a bit later was one of the odder things about this shadowy war. Roads were safe one day, suicide the next. Warlords thought to be relatively trustworthy one week were reported to have personally overseen the meticulous looting of an aid-group warehouse the next. All of this seemed designed to prevent anyone from actually fighting. From the little Donk had seen and heard, gun battles here seemed founded upon one's ability to spray bullets blindly around rocks and walls and then beat a quick, spectacular retreat.

"How do you feel?" Donk asked Graves now.

Graves, still sitting on the bumper, flashed his ruined teeth. The dirty wind had given his eyes a teary under-rim. "How do I look?"

"Fading. We need to get you somewhere."

Graves looked down, angrily blinking away his eyes' moisture. "Where are we, anyway?"

"About an hour outside Kunduz."

"That's another hour from Mazar?"

"Roughly."

Graves glanced around, but the dunes were too high to see anything but the road and the road was too straight to reveal anything but the dunes. "Not far enough, I imagine."

"Probably not."

"We could hitch. Someone is bound to be along."

"Someone is. *Who* is the problem."

"You don't think the poor devils would use *roads,* for God's sake, do you? This far north? They'd be bombed within minutes."

"I have no idea."

With shiatsu delicacy, Graves massaged his face with his fingertips. A bright bracelet of untanned flesh encircled his wrist. Graves's watch, too, had been stolen. His hands fell into his lap, then, and he sighed. "I hope you're not worried, Duncan."

Donk decided not to remind Graves, for what would have been the fortieth time, that he preferred to be called Donk. The nickname—a diminutive form of *donkey*—dated to one of the boyhood camping trips he and his father and older brother Jason used to take every year in the Porcupine Mountains of Michigan's Upper Peninsula. If he had never especially liked the name, he had come to understand himself through its drab prism. DONK ST. PIERRE was stamped in raised black type upon his ivory business card; it was the name above which his photographs were published. People often mistook his work for that of some Flemish eccentric. When colleagues first met him, something Donk called The Moment inescapably came to pass. Faced not with a tall, spectral, chain-smoking European but a short, overweight Midwesterner with frizzy black hair and childlishly small hands, their smiles faded, their eyes crumpled, and a discreet little sound died just past their glottis.

"I'm not worried," Donk said. "I'll be even less worried when we figure out where we're going."

Graves stared at Donk as though weighing him in some crucial balance. "You seemed rather jittery in Pyanj. Wasn't sure you'd be up to this."

When Donk said nothing Graves stood, listing momentarily before he steadied himself against the Corolla with one hand. Hassan loped back over to them, grinning beneath the pressure of one of his patented "discoveries," always uncanny in their relative uselessness. "My friends, I have discovered that nearby there is village. Good village,

12

the driver says. Safe, friendly village. We will be welcome there. He told for me the way. Seven, eight kilometers."

Although this was much better information than Hassan was usually able to manage, Graves's expression was sour. Sweat dripped off his nose, and he was breathing hard. Merely standing had wiped him out. "Did he tell you that, or did you ask him?"

Hassan seemed puzzled. "I ask-ed him. Why?"

"Because, Hassan, information is only as reliable as the question that creates it."

"Mister Graves, I am not understanding you."

"He's saying," Donk said, "that our wheat-stealing friend may be telling us to go somewhere we shouldn't."

Hassan looked at them both in horror. "My friends, *no*. This is not possible. He is good man. And we are gracious, hospitable people here. We would never—"

Graves, cruelly, was ignoring this. "How's the car?"

Donk shook his head. "Wheel won't turn, engine won't start. Back wheels are buried in sand. And there's the windshield issue. Other than that, it's ready to go."

Graves walked out into the middle of the highway, drawing the blanket up over his head. Each end of the road streaked off into a troubling desert nothingness and appeared to tunnel into the horizon itself. It was hours before noon in northern Afghanistan, and the country felt as empty and skull-white as a moon. Not our familiar moon but another, harder, stranger moon. Above, the clouds were like little white bubbles of soap that had been incompletely sponged off the hard slate of the blue morning sky. Donk was compelled to wonder if nothingness and trouble were not, in fact, indistinguishable. Graves marched back over to the Corolla and savagely yanked his duffel from the front seat. "We walk to this village, then."

When it became apparent to the driver that they were leaving, he spoke up, clearly agitated. Hassan translated. "He says he won't leave his car."

"I don't blame him," Graves said, and peeled off three twenties to pay the man.

After leaving the main highway, they walked along a scarred, inattentively paved road toward the village Hassan had promised was only six or seven or was it eleven kilometers away. Human Conflict, Donk thought, rather abstractly. It was one of his lively but undisciplined mind's fascinations. It differed from land to land, as faces differed. But the basic elements (ears, nose, mouth; aid workers, chaos, exhilaration) were always the same. It was the one thing that survived every era, every philosophy, the one legacy each civilization surrendered to the next. For Donk, Human Conflict was curiously life-affirming, based as it was on avoiding death—indeed, on inflicting death preemptively on others. He loved Human Conflict not as an ideal but as a milieu, a state of mind one absorbed but was not absorbed by, the crucial difference between combatants and non-. His love of Human Conflict was as unapologetic as it was without nuance. He simply *enjoyed* it. "Duncan," a therapist had once asked him, "have you ever heard of the term *chronic habitual suicide*?" Donk never saw that therapist, or any other, again.

He kicked from his path a billiard-ball-sized chunk of concrete. How was it that these people, the Afghans, could, for two hundred years, hold off or successfully evade several of the world's most go-getting empires and not find it within themselves to pave a fucking road? And yet somehow Afghanistan was, at least for the time being, the world's most significant place. Human Conflict had a way of doing that too. He remembered a press conference two weeks ago in the Presidential Palace in Tashkent, the capital of neighboring Uzbekistan, where the fragrant, rested-looking journalists who had arrived with the American secretary of state had surrounded him. Donk had taken his establishing shots of the secretary—looking determined and unusually Vulcan behind his press-conference podium—and quickly withdrawn. In one of the palace's uninhabited corners he found a splendid globe as large as an underwater mine, all of its countries' names in Cyrillic. Central Asia was turned out toward the room; North America faced the wall. Seeing the planet displayed from that strange side had seemed to Donk as mistaken as an upside-down letter. But it was not wrong. That globe was in fact perfectly accurate.

Up ahead, Graves was walking more slowly now, almost shuffling. Donk was allowing Graves the lead largely because Graves needed the lead. He was one of those rare people one did not actually mind seeing take charge. But Graves, wrapped in his red blanket, looked little better than a confused pensioner. The sun momentarily withdrew behind one of the bigger bubbly cloud formations. The temperature dropped with shocking immediacy, the air suddenly as sharp as angel hair. Donk watched Graves's bootlaces come slowly and then floppily untied. For some reason Donk was too embarrassed for Graves to say anything.

"Mister Donk," Hassan said quietly, drawing beside him. "Is Mister Graves all right?"

Donk managed a weak, testy smile. "Mister Graves is fine."

Hassan nodded. "May I, Mister Donk, ask you questions?"

"You may."

"Where were you born in America?"

"Near the Sea of Tranquillity."

"I ask, what is your favorite food?"

"Blueberry filling."

"American women are very beautiful, they say. They say too they have much love."

"That's mostly true. You should only sleep with beautiful women, even though they have the least love. Write that down. With women it's all confidence, Hassan. Write that down too. You might look at me and think, But this is a fat man! And it's true. But I grow on people. You're not writing."

"I hear that American women make many demands. Not like Afghan women."

"Did you steal my cameras?"

"Mister Donk! No!"

"That's not nice, you know," Graves said suddenly, glancing back. "Teasing the boy like that."

"I was wondering when I'd get your attention."

"Leave the boy alone, Duncan. He's dealt with enough bad information to last his entire lifetime."

"I am not a boy," Hassan said suddenly.

"Don't listen to him," Graves said to Hassan. "War's made Mister Duncan barmy."

"How are you feeling?" Donk asked Graves. "Any better?"

Graves dropped his eyes to his open palm. "I was just checking my cell phone again. Nothing." Some enigma of telecommunications had prevented his Nokia from functioning the moment they crossed into Afghanistan. He tried absently to put away the phone but missed his pocket. Graves stopped and stared at the Nokia, a plastic purple amethyst half buried in the sand. Donk scooped it up and handed it back to Graves, who nodded distantly. Suddenly the sky filled with a deep, nearly divine roar. Their three heads simultaneously tipped back. Nothing. American F/A-18s and F-14s were somewhere cutting through that high blue, releasing satellite- and laser-guided bombs or returning from dropping bombs or looking for new places to drop bombs. Graves shook his head, quick and hard, as though struggling to believe that these jets really existed. Only after the roar faded did they push on, all of them now walking Wizard-of-Oz abreast. Graves still seemed angry.

"Sometimes," he said, "I wonder if all the oil companies and the American military purposefully create these fucking crises to justify launching all those pretty missiles and dropping all these dreadful, expensive bombs. Air Force. Error Farce is more like it."

"Coalition troops," Donk reminded him. "Those could be British jets."

"Somehow, Duncan, I doubt that."

Donk swigged from his canteen and wiped his mouth with his forearm. Talking politics with Graves was like being handed an armful of eels and then being asked to pretend that they were bunnies. He did not typically mind arguing, certainly not with a European, especially about the relative merits of the Land of the Red, White, and Blue. But Graves did not seem up to it. Donk settled on what he hoped was a slightly less divisive topic. "I wonder if they caught him yet."

"They're not going to catch him. The first private from Iowa to find him is going to push him up against a cave wall and blow a hole in his skull." Graves seemed unable to take his eyes off his feet.

"Well," Donk said, "let's hope so."

Graves looked over at him with lucid, gaunt-faced disappointment. He snorted and returned his gaze to his All-Stars, their red fabric so dusty they now appeared pink. "I can't believe someone as educated as you would think that's appropriate."

"I'm not that educated." Donk noted that Graves was practically panting, his mouth open and his tongue peeking over the fence post of his lower front teeth. Donk touched him on the shoulder. "Graves, hey. You really look like you need to rest again."

Graves's reaction was to nod, stop, and collapse into a rough squat, his legs folding beneath him at an ugly, painful-looking angle. Donk handed Graves his canteen while Hassan, standing nearby, mashed some raisins into his mouth. Graves watched a chewing Hassan watch him for a while, then closed his eyes. "My head," he said. "Suddenly it's splitting."

"Malaria," Donk said, kneeling next to him. "The symptoms are cyclical. Headaches. Fever. Chills. The sweats."

"Yes," Graves said heavily. "I know. Until the little buggers have clogged my blood vessels. Goodbye, vital organs."

"Malaria isn't fatal," Donk said.

Graves shook his head. It occurred to Donk that Graves's face, which tapered slightly at his temples and swelled again at his jawline, was shaped rather like a foot. "Untreated malaria is often fatal."

Donk looked at him evenly. Graves's thermal underwear top had soaked through. The sharp curlicues of grayish hair that swirled in the hollow of Graves's throat sparkled with sweat. His skin was shinier than his eyes by quite a lot.

"Tell me something," Graves said suddenly. "Why were you so nervous-seeming in Pyanj?"

Donk sighed. "Because nothing was happening. When nothing is happening I get jumpy."

Graves nodded quickly. "I heard that about you."

"You did?"

"That was a splendid shot, you know. The dead Tajik woman in Dushanbe. Brains still leaking from her head. You were there—what—three minutes after she was shot? I wonder, though. Do you see her when you sleep, Duncan?"

It was probably Donk's most famous photo, and his first real one. The woman had been gunned down by Russian soldiers in the Tajik capital during an early ugly paroxysm of street fighting. The Russians were in Tajikistan as peacekeepers after the Soviet collapse. Her death had been an accident, cross fire. She had known people were fighting on that street, but she walked down it anyway. You saw a lot of that in urban warfare. Chronic habitual suicide. In the photo her groceries were scattered beside her. One of her shoes was missing. A bit of her brain in the snow—just a bit, as though it were some glistening red fruit that had been spooned onto a bed of sugar—the rest shining wetly in a dark black gash just above her ear. Her mouth was open. The photo had run on the wires all over the world and, from what he had heard, infuriated the Russian authorities, which explained the difficulty he always had getting into Russia. "I guess I'm not a very haunted person," Donk said finally.

Graves was still smiling in a manner Donk recognized for its casual hopelessness. It was a war-zone look. He had seen it on aid workers' faces and correspondents' faces but most often on soldiers' faces. He had witnessed it, too, on the bearded faces of the POWs in Kunduz's granary. Hassan had stopped eating his raisins and now watched the two men. He saw the look too—perhaps because, Donk thought, it was his own default expression.

"But you love death, though, Duncan, yes?" Graves asked. "You have to. We all do. That's why we do this, isn't it?"

Donk began to pat himself down in search of something. He did not know what. He disliked such emotional nudism. He stopped pawing himself then, and, feeling not a little caught out, traced his finger around in the sand. He made a peace sign, an easy shape to make. "Graves, I have learned not to generalize much about people in our line of work. The best combat photographer I ever knew was the mother of two children."

"Russian?"

"Israeli."

Graves leaned forward slightly. "Do you know what Montaigne says?"

Donk neither moved nor breathed nor blinked. He heard *Montaigne* as *Montane*. "Can we walk again now?"

"Montaigne believed that death was easiest for those who thought about it the most. That way it was possible for a man to die resigned. 'The utility of living consists not in the length of days'—Montaigne said this—'but in the use of time.'" Graves smiled again.

Donk decided to switch tacks. "Your Royal Illness," he said cheerfully, getting to his feet, "I bid you, rise and walk."

Graves merely sat there, shivering. His khaki vest looked two sizes too large for him, his hair no longer so thick-looking now that it was soaked to his skull, his snowy scalp showing through. Graves seemed reduced, as unsightly as a wet rodent. "Isn't it strange," he asked, "that in the midst of all this a man can die from a mosquito bite?"

Donk's voice hardened. "*A,* Graves, give me a break. *B,* You're not going to die."

He laughed, lightly. "Today, no. Probably not."

Donk had a thought. *Deborah. Turn the toaster.* This Deborah had to be Graves's girlfriend or common-law wife. The man did not seem traditional husband material, somehow. "Graves, you need to walk. For Deborah."

Graves's puzzled face lifted up, and for a moment he looked his imperious self again. "Who the devil is Deborah?"

"Mister Donk—" Hassan said urgently, all but pulling on Donk's sleeve.

"Graves," Donk said, "I *need* you to get *up.*"

Graves lay back, alone in his pain, his skull finding the pillow of his duffel bag. "It's my head, Duncan. I can't bloody *think.*"

"Mister Donk!" Hassan said, but it was too late. The jeep was approaching in a cloud of dust.

＝＝

The owner of the jeep was a thirtyish man named Ahktar. He wore blue jeans and a thin gray windbreaker and, as it happened, was only lightly armed, outwardly friendly, and claimed to live in the village they were headed toward. It was his "delight," he said, to give them a ride. He spoke a little English. "My father," he explained, once they were moving along, "is chief of my village. I go to school in Mazar city, where I learn English at the English Club."

"You're a student now?" Donk asked, surprised. He found he could not stop looking at Ahktar's thick mustache and toupee-shaped hair, both as impossibly black as photocopier ink.

He laughed. "No. Many years ago."

Hassan and Donk bounced around on the jeep's stiff backseat as Ahktar took them momentarily off-road, avoiding a dune that had drifted out into the highway. Jumper cables and needle-nose pliers jangled around at Donk's feet. Graves was seat-belted in the shotgun position next to Ahktar, jostling in the inert manner of a crash-test dummy. Donk had yet to find the proper moment to ask why in Afghanistan the steering wheels were found on the right side of the car when everyone drove on the right side of the road. He thought he had found that moment now but, before he could ask, Ahktar hit a bump and Donk bashed his head against the vehicle's metal roof. "Your jeep," Donk said, rubbing his head through his terrorist-style do-rag.

"Good jeep!" Ahktar said.

"It's a little . . . military-seeming."

Ahktar looked at him in the rearview and shook his head. He had not heard him.

Donk leaned forward. "Military!" he shouted over the jeep's gruff lawn-mowerish engine. "It looks like you got it from the military!"

"Yes, yes," Ahktar said, clearly humoring Donk. "I do!"

Donk leaned back. "This *is* a military jeep, isn't it?" he asked Hassan.

"His father maybe is warlord," Hassan offered. "A good warlord!"

"Where are you from?" Ahktar asked Donk. "America?"

"That's right," Donk said.

"You know Lieutenant Marty?" Ahktar asked.

"Lieutenant Marty? No, I'm sorry. I don't."

Ahktar seemed disappointed. "Captain Herb?"

"No. Why do you ask?"

Ahktar reached into the side pocket of his gray coat and handed back to Donk a slip of paper with the names *Captain Herb* and *Lieutenant Marty* written on it, above what looked to be a pi-length satellite phone number. "Who are they?" Donk asked, handing the paper back.

"American soldiers," he said happily. "We are friends now because I help them with some problems."

"Is there a phone in your village? We could call them."

"Sorry, no," Ahktar apologized. "We have radios in my village but nearest phone is Kunduz. I think today I will not go to Kunduz. They are having problems there." He motioned toward Graves, who seemed to be napping. "From where in America is your friend?"

"I'm not an American," Graves muttered, with as much force as Donk had heard him manage all day. "I'm *English.*"

"What?" Ahktar asked, leaning toward him.

Graves's eyes cracked open, dim and sticky like a newborn's. "I'm *English.* From England. The people your countrymen butchered by the thousand a hundred and fifty years ago."

"Yes," Ahktar said soberly, downshifting as they came to a hill. Something in the jeep's heater was rattling like a playing card in bicycle spokes. The waves of air surging from its vents went from warm, to hot, to freezing, to hot again. Ahktar drew up in his seat. "Here is village."

As they plunged down the highway, hazy purple mountains materialized along the horizon. From the road's rise, Ahktar's village appeared as an oblong smear of homes and buildings located just before a flattened area where the mountain range's foothills began. Now came a new low-ground terrain covered with scrabbly, drought-ruined grass. Along the road were dozens of wireless and long-knocked-over telephone poles. The jeep rolled through the village's outer checkpoint. Set back off the highway, every fifty yards, were some small stone bubble-domed homes, their chimneys smoking. They looked to Donk like prehistoric arboretums. None of it was like anything Donk had ever before seen in Central Asia. The virus of Soviet architecture—with its ballpark right angles, frail plaster, and monstrous frescoes—had not spread here. In the remoter villages of Tajikistan he had seen poverty to rival northern Afghanistan's, but there the Soviet center had always held. In these never-mastered lands south of the former Soviet border, everything appeared old and shot up and grievously unattended. These discrepancies reminded Donk of what borders really meant and what, for better or worse, they protected.

The road narrowed. The houses grew tighter, bigger,

and slightly taller. The smoky air thickened, and soon they were rolling through Ahktar's village proper. He saw a few shops crammed with junk—ammunition and foodstuffs and Aladdin's lamp for all he knew—their window displays tiered backward like auditorium seating. Black curly-haired goats hoofed at the dirt. Dogs slunk from doorway to doorway. Dark hawk-nosed men wearing shirts with huge floppy sleeves waved at Ahktar. Most looked Tajik, and Donk cursed his laziness for not learning at least how to count in Tajik during all the months he had spent in Tajikistan. Walking roadside were beehive-shaped figures whose bedspread-white and sky-blue garments managed to hide even the basest suggestion of human form. These were women. Around their facial areas Donk noted narrow, tightly latticed eye slots. Children ran happily beside the jeep, many holding pieces of taut string. "Kites," Graves observed weakly. "They're flying kites."

Ahktar's face turned prideful. "Now we are free, you see." He pointed at the sky. Donk turned his head sideways and peered up out the window. Floating above the low buildings of Ahktar's village were, indeed, scores of kites. Some were boxes, others quadrangular; some swooped and weaved like osprey, others hung eerily suspended.

Hassan looked up also. "We could not fly kites before," he said quietly.

"Yes," Donk said. "I know. Let freedom ring."

"When they leave our village," Ahktar—a bit of a present-tense addict, it seemed—went on, "we see many changes, such as shaving of the beards. The men used to grow big beards, of course very long, and they checked!"

Donk smiled. "So you had a long beard?"

"Of course I have. I show you my pictures. It was a very long beard! Now everybody is free to shave or grow as their own choice."

It seemed impious to point out that virtually every man momentarily centered within the frame of Donk's murky plastic window had a griffin's nest growing off his chin.

"When did they leave?" Donk asked. "Was it recently?"

"Oh, yes," Ahktar said. "Very recently!" He cut the engine and rolled them down a rough dirt path through a part of the village that seemed a stone labyrinth. Sack-burdened peasants struggled past plain mud homes. Kunduz suddenly seemed a thriving desert metropolis in comparison. A high-walled compound guarded by two robed young men cradling Kalashnikovs stood where the path dwindled into a driveway. Inches before the compound's metal gate the jeep rolled to a soft stop. Ahktar climbed out of the vehicle, and Donk followed.

"What's this?" Donk asked.

"My father's house. I think you are in trouble. If so, he is the man you are wanting to talk to now."

"We're not in trouble," Donk said. "My friend is sick. We just need to get him some medicine. We're not in any trouble. Our car broke down."

Ahktar lifted his hands, as though to ease Donk. "Yes, yes." He moved toward the compound's gate. "Come. Follow."

"What about my friend?" But Donk turned to see that the guards were helping Graves from the jeep and leading him toward Ahktar's father's compound. Surprisingly, Graves did not spurn their assistance or call them bloody Hindoos, but simply nodded and allowed his arms to find their way around each guard's neck. They dragged him along, Graves's legs serving as occasional steadying kickstands. Hassan followed behind them, again nervously eating the raisins he kept in his pocket.

The large courtyard, its trees stripped naked by autumn, was patrolled by a dozen more men holding Kalashnikovs. They were decked out in the same crossbred battle dress as the soldiers Donk had seen loitering around Kunduz: camouflage pants so recently issued by the American military they still held their crease, shiny black boots, *pakul*s (the floppy national hat of Afghanistan), rather grandmotherly shawls, and shiny leather bandoliers. While most of the bandoliers were empty, a few of these irregulars had hung upon them three or four small bulblike grenades. They looked a little like explosive human Christmas trees.

"Wait one moment, please," Ahktar said, strolling across the courtyard and ducking into one of the many dark doorless portals at its northern edge. The guards deposited Graves at a wooden table, and a minute later he was brought a pot of tea. Donk and Hassan, exchanging glances, walked over to Graves's table and sat down in the cold dark light. The soldiers on the compound's periphery had yet to acknowledge them. They simply walked back and forth, back and forth, along the walls. Something about their manner, simultaneously alert and robotic, led Donk to guess that their weapons' safeties were off—if Kalashnikovs even *had* safeties, which, come to think of it, he was fairly sure they did not.

"Nothing quite like a safe, friendly village," Graves said in a thin voice. He sipped his tea, holding the round handleless cup with both hands.

"How do you feel, Mister Graves?" Hassan asked eagerly.

"Hassan, I feel dreadful."

"I'm sorry to hear this, Mister Graves."

Graves set down the teacup and frowned. He looked at Hassan. "Be a lad and see if you can't scare up some sugar for me, would you?"

Hassan stared at him, empty-faced.

Graves chuckled at the moment he seemed to recognize that the joke had not been funny. "I'm joking, Hassan." He poured them both a cup of tea, and with a dramatic shiver quickly returned his arm to the warm protective folds of his blanket. "Bloody freezing, isn't it?"

"It's actually a little warmer," Donk said, turning from his untouched tea to see Ahktar and an older gentleman walking over to join them. Ahktar's father was a towering man with a great napkin-shaped cinnamon beard. He wore long clean white-yellow robes and a leather belt as thick as a cummerbund. Stuffed into this belt was what looked to be a .45. He was almost certainly Tajik, and had large crazed eyes and a nose that looked as hard as a sharp growth of bark. But he was smiling—something he did not do well, possibly for lack of practice. When he was close he threw open his arms and proclaimed something with an air of highly impersonal sympathy.

"My father says you are welcome," Ahktar said. He did not much resemble his father, being smaller and darker-skinned. Doubtless Ahktar had a Pashtun mother around here somewhere. Donk could almost assemble her features. His father said something else, then nudged Ahktar to translate. "He says too that you are his great and protected guests." His father spoke again, still with his effortful smile. "He says he is grateful for American soldiers and grateful for you American journalists, who care only of the truth."

"English," Graves said quietly.

"Whatever trouble you are in my father will help you. It is his delight."

"Ahktar." Donk stepped in gently, "I told you. We're not in any trouble. My friend here is very sick. Our car broke down. We were trying to go to Mazar. It's very simple."

Ahktar said nothing.

"Well," Donk asked, "are you going to tell your father that?"

"I tell him that already."

"Then can we go to Mazar from here?"

The muscles of Ahktar's face tightened with regret. "Unfortunately, that is problem. No one is going to Mazar today." He seemed suddenly to wish that he were not standing beside his father, who of course asked what had just been said. Ahktar quietly back-translated for him, obviously hoping that his pea of an answer would be smothered beneath the mattress of translation.

"Why can't we go to Mazar?" Donk pressed.

At this mention of Mazar his father spoke again, angrily now. Ahktar nodded obediently. "My father wishes you to know you are safe here. Mazar is maybe not so safe."

"But Mazar's perfectly safe. It's been safe for days. I have friends there."

"My father is friendly with American soldiers in Mazar. Very friendly. And now we are helping them with some problems they are having in this region. We have authority for this. Unfortunately, Mazar's Uzbek commander and my father are not very friendly, and there my father has no authority. Therefore it would be good for you to stay."

After a pause, Donk spoke. "Who, may I ask, is your father?"

"My father is General Ismail Mohammed. He was very important part of United National Islamic Front for the Salvation of Afghanistan, which fought against—"

"But Mazar's commander was part of that same front."

"Yes," Ahktar said sadly. "Here is problem."

Donk had met a suspiciously large number of generals during his time in Afghanistan, and was not sure how to judge General Mohammed's significance. Warlord? Ally? Both? He let it drop. "Do you have medicine here?"

Again Ahktar shrugged. "Some. But unfortunately it is with my father's soldiers now. They are out taking care of some problems for Lieutenant Marty."

"Is Lieutenant Marty with them?"

"Oh, no. Lieutenant Marty is in Mazar."

"Where we can't go."

"Yes."

There really were, Donk had often thought, and thought again now, two kinds of people in the world: Chaos People and Order People. For Donk this was not a bit of cynical Kipling wisdom to be doled out among fellow journalists in barren Inter-Continental barrooms. It was not meant in a condescending way. No judgment; it was a purely empirical matter: Chaos People, Order People. Anyone who doubted this had never tried to wait in line, board a plane, or get off a bus among Chaos People. The next necessary division of the world's people took place along the lines of whether they actually knew what they were. The Japanese were Order People and knew it. Americans and English were Chaos People who thought they were Order People. The French were the worst thing to be: Order People who thought they were Chaos People. But Afghans, like Africans and Russians and the Irish, were Chaos People who knew they were Chaos People, and while this lent them a good amount of charm, it made their countries berserk, insane. Countries did indeed go insane. Sometimes they went insane and stayed insane. Chaos People's countries particularly tended to stay insane. Donk miserably pulled off his do-rag, the bloody glue that held the fabric to his skin tearing from his ruined eyebrow so painfully that he had to work to keep the tears from his eyes. "So tell me, Ahktar. What are we supposed to do here?"

Before anyone could answer, Graves had a seizure.

A few hours later, Donk was sitting outside the room in which Graves had been all but quarantined. He was petting a stray wolfish mongrel with filaments of silver hair threaded through its black coat, waiting for the village medicine man to emerge from Graves's room. This man had claimed he was a doctor and offered up to Donk a large pouch of herbs as evidence. Donk did not have the heart to argue. The compound was quiet, except for some small animals fighting or playing along the eaves just above Donk's head and the occasional overhead roar of a jet. Hassan, sitting a few feet away, watched Donk stroke the dog's head in revulsion.

"Why," he asked finally, "do you do that?"

Donk had always taken pity on Central Asian dogs, especially after learning that one could fend off a possible attack by miming the act of picking up a stone, at which the dogs usually turned and ran away. He lowered his lips to the creature's head and planted upon it a chaste kiss. The dog smelled of oily musk. "Because it's lonely," Donk said.

"That is a filthy animal," Hassan told him. "You should not touch such a filthy animal, Mister Donk."

Donk chose not to point out that Hassan was, if anything, far dirtier. The boy had spent a night with Donk and Graves in Kunduz. His body odor had been so potent, so overwhelmingly cheesy, that Donk had not been able to sleep. Misplaced Muslim piety, he thought with uncharacteristic bitterness.

33

"You're right," Donk said at last. "The dog's filthy. But so am I. So there we are."

Hassan *hmph*ed.

During the seizure Donk had stuffed his bloody do-rag in Graves's mouth to keep him from biting off his tongue, even though he knew convulsive people rarely, if ever, bit off their own tongues. It was one of those largely ceremonial things people did in emergencies. Donk had pushed Graves up on the table and held him down. Graves shuddered for a few moments, his eyes filled with awful awareness, his chest heaving like the gills of a suffocating fish. Then, mercifully, he went unconscious. Donk used the rest of his iodined water to try to rehydrate Graves, but he quickly vomited it up. At this General Mohammed had sent for his medicine man.

Donk knew there were at least two kinds of malaria. The less serious strain was stubborn and hard to kill—flulike symptoms could recur as long as five decades after the initial infection—but it was rarely lethal. The more serious strain quickly turned life-threatening if untreated. He was no longer wondering which strain Graves had contracted. Graves was conscious now—Donk could hear him attempting to reason with the village doctor—but his voice was haggard and dazed.

Donk looked around. Thirty or forty yards away a small group of General Mohammed's soldiers watched him, their Kalashnikovs slung over their shoulders. They looked beaten, bullied, violent. Hair-trigger men. Their faces were like shadows. And these were the *winners*. Donk found himself, suddenly, missing women. Seeing them, staring at them, smelling them. Afghanistan had mailed into Donk's brain a series of crushingly similar mental postcards: men, men, desert, men, men, men, guns, men, guns, guns, desert, guns, men. One might think that life without women would lead to a simpler, less fraught existence. No worries about hair or odor. Saying whatever you wanted. But one's eye tired of men as surely as one's nerves tired of guns.

It was not just women, however. Donk missed sex even more. He needed, he admitted, an inordinate amount of sex. Heavy people needed things—hence their heaviness. Sex was a large part of the reason he had been reluctant to leave Chicago to come to Afghanistan. He was having a Guinness Book amount of it with Tina, who was maybe his girlfriend, his first in a long time. As luck would have it, Tina was menstruating the night before he left. They had had sex anyway, in her bathroom, and left bloody foot- and handprints all over the white tile. They Windexed away the blood together. It had not been freaky. It had almost been beautiful, and he loved her. But for him distance was permission, and newness arousal itself. Plane tickets and hotel rooms were like lingerie. He had already slept with an AP reporter in Tashkent. He did not regret it, exactly, because he had every intention of lying about it later. It occurred to him that he had also lied to Graves, about not being haunted. Strangely, he felt bad about that lie. It seemed like something Graves should have known. But Donk had not known where to begin.

A decade ago, Donk had worked as a staff photographer for a dozen family newspapers peppered throughout central Wisconsin, all somehow owned by the same unmarried Republican. His life then had been sitting through school-board meetings and upping the wattage of the smiles of local luminaries, drinking three-dollar pitchers of Bud after work, and suffering polite rejection from strangers he misjudged as unattractive enough to want to speak to him. This life began to end when the last of five sudden strokes stripped Donk's father of his mind and sent him off into dementia. Donk was the only one of his siblings who lived within a thousand miles of Milwaukee, where his father was hospitalized; his mother had long refused to speak to the man. So, alone, Donk had set up camp beside his father's deathbed.

Death was a peculiar thing. Some people endured unenviable amounts of firsthand death without its one clearest implication ever occurring to them. Donk had never much thought about his own death before. The prospect had always felt to him like a television show he knew was on channel 11 at eight o'clock but had never watched and never planned to. Donk stared at the monitors, listened to the hiss of his father's bed's mattress as the nurses pistoned it up and down, timed the steady beep whose provenance he did not care to isolate. It was all he could do to keep from thinking that everything was assembled to provide the man a few last deprived moments of life. Donk realized that even if he were beside his father at the moment his final journey began, the man would still die alone, as Donk would die alone, as we all die alone. Horribly, doubly alone, for just as no one went with us, no one greeted us when it was over.

Nurses found him weeping in the hospital's cafeteria. When his father's doctor brought some final forms for Donk to fill out, she slipped into his catatonic hand a small packet of diazepam. The nervous breakdown, Donk expected. The estrangement from his surviving family—who could not understand his "sudden obsession" with dying—he expected. Quitting his job and investing his small inheritance, he expected; becoming a freelance combat photographer, he did not. People who were not correspondents laughed when Donk told the story, which he often did. It sounded so unbelievable. But people are not born combat photographers any more than they are born lawyers. One day you were waiting tables; the next you were in law school. One day you were heartbroken and megalomaniacal; the next you were faxing visa requests to embassies using stolen letterhead. Only Tajikistan's had answered him. If Tajikistan's embassy wondered why the *Waukesha Freeman* felt it needed a photographer in Dushanbe, it did not share that curiosity with Donk. He was awarded his first visa to his first war, a genuine hot war, a civil war. He told everyone he met in Dushanbe that he was "stringing," even though he was not sure what that word really entailed. In Tajikistan he saw his first gunshot wound, his first dead baby. He learned that combat photographers either spooked or did not. To his surprise, Donk did not. At least, he spooked no more than on the afternoon he watched his father burp, sigh, and stop breathing. The photo of the gunned-down old woman, taken after five months and $3,000 of squandered savings, led to Donk's covering the reconciliation trials in Rwanda for one of India's biggest dailies. There he learned that he no longer had much patience for American minorities' claims of oppression. Rwanda led to Jerusalem, shortly after the intifada. There he learned of the subterranean connections world media outlets had expertly tunneled beneath continents of human misery, and how often you passed the same faces when traveling through them. Jerusalem led to Dagestan, where he spent a day with a Tatar Muslim warlord whose nom de guerre was Hitler and who made an awkward pass at Donk when they were alone. He learned that, of all the countries in the world, America was most hesitant to publish graphic "bang-bang" photos. He learned that arms and cocaine were the world's second and third most profitable exports, after human sex slaves. He learned how to shop for a Kevlar vest. He learned how to take a good picture while running. He learned, when all else failed, to follow refugees. And he learned that the worse and more ugly the reality around him, and the more impervious to it and better he felt, the more he forgot his father. He learned that the only thing that truly frightened him was quiet, because he knew death was quiet—the longest quiet. He learned that the persona that came with this strange fearlessness was able to win, if only for a night, a certain kind of troubled heart belonging to a certain kind of woman more worldly than Donk had any previous right to expect, and he learned that he was the type of man to abuse this ability.

His brother and sister called him a fear addict, a desperate idiot on a danger bender; they claimed he had never "dealt" with their father's death. Donk's brother,

Jason, was a first-team whiskey addict (three interventions and counting: "What, this again?" he had asked, after the most recent). His sister, Marie, lived in Anchorage, too far away to provide Donk with any idea of what, exactly, she was into. Judging from her insensate 3 a.m. phone calls, it was high-impact. Who were they to speak of fear, of "dealing with the natural process of death"? Death was actually the least natural thing Donk could imagine, involving, as it did, not living. Death's stature as a physiological event did not mean it was natural. The trapped mink does not accept its own death; it chews off its leg. No, death was something else, uncategorized and dreadful, something to be fought off, defied, spat upon. Human Conflict, he thought. Death was the unappeasable aggressor. And he stroked the dog's small head.

The medicine man stepped from Graves's room. Without consulting him, Donk rushed inside. It was a little past ten in the morning now, the light in Graves's room brighter than he expected. Graves was supine on a thick mass of blankets with another, thinner blanket mostly covering him. He seemed very still. His eyes were dry. Though he did not look at Donk, he raised his hand in brief acknowledgment. Donk crouched next to Graves's makeshift bed and said nothing. Then, on an impulse, he took Graves's hand and held it crossways in his own, as though hoping to offer him some mysterious transfer of strength.

"Did you once think," Graves asked, "about how dirty dying is? I'm lying here in my own shit. You can smell it, can't you? I should really do something about this." He shifted positions and Donk did smell Graves's shit, thin and sour and soupy. In response he squeezed Graves's hand. "In England," Graves went on, wincing briefly, "I think something like eighty percent of all deaths now take place in hospitals. I watched my mother and my father die in hospitals. They went quietly. It was lovely, in its way. But fifty years ago only forty percent of the English population died in hospitals. We sequester the dying, you see. Because it *is* ugly, it *is* dirty. I think we don't want to know that. We want to keep that little truth hidden away. But think a moment about how most people have died, Duncan. They've died in places just like this. So if I'm going to die here I'm joining legions. For some reason this makes me happy." Graves's head rolled an inch on its pillow, and, for the first time, he looked at Donk.

Donk stared back at Graves, the connection allowing him to locate the voice, as faraway as a quasar, in his mind. "You're not going to die."

Graves smiled. "Old men have to die. The world grows moldy, otherwise."

Graves, Donk knew, was forty. His sympathy left him in one brash gust. "What did the doctor say?"

"Oh, you mean St. John's Wort, MD? Hell if I know. He all but sprinkled me with voodoo dust. Duncan, calm down. I'm either going to make it through this or I won't. I'm not upset. I just have to wait." He closed his eyes. "'Of all the wonders that I yet have heard, / It seems to me most strange that men should fear; / Seeing that death, a necessary end, / Will come when it will come.' That Shakespeare. Preternatural, isn't it? Any occasion one can think of, and there he is."

Donk knew he could barely quote Shakespeare if he were spotted "To be" and "not to be." In a low voice he said, "You *are* going to die, Graves, if you've already convinced yourself you're going to die."

"A puzzle."

Donk let go of his hand. "It's not a fucking puzzle."

"Getting upset, Duncan, isn't going to help me."

"Then what *is* going to help you?"

"Medicine. Medicine they don't have here."

"Where?" Donk asked. "Where do I go?"

Graves looked at him again. Suddenly Donk saw the fear just below the flat blue composure of Graves's eyes, a stern, dignified terror barricaded so completely inside of him it barely recognized itself. Graves's lips were shaking. "Jesus, Duncan. I—you—you could rent that chap Ahktar's jeep. You could—"

With that Donk rushed out, collared Hassan, and went to find General Mohammed and Ahktar. Seven hundred dollars was hidden beneath the insole of Donk's boot. This would be enough, he hoped, for a safety deposit on the jeep. He would drive to Mazar with Hassan. He would walk into UNICEF's office or Doctors Without Borders or find Lieutenant Marty and he would come back here. Graves was too sick to travel, and if they broke down again or were stopped—it was too complicated. That was the one truly upsetting thing about Human Conflict: It made everything far too complicated.

Donk found General Mohammed alone in his quarters. He was wearing glasses, surprisingly enough, sitting at a plain wooden desk, reading a book in Persian. His .45

was flat on the tabletop. Behind the general, on the wall, hung a green-and-black flag last used in Afghanistan during the reign of its deposed king, thirty years ago. Without knocking, Donk announced he was renting Ahktar's jeep and going to Mazar. Without looking up, General Mohammed informed him that Ahktar had, only an hour before, left in his jeep to take care of a few more problems. He would be back sometime tomorrow, perhaps maybe. Donk stood silently by the general's doorjamb, feeling himself growing smaller. *Perhaps maybe.* The national motto of Afghanistan.

"He says," Hassan translated for General Mohammed, "that Mister Graves is very sick. He says he has spoken to his doctor."

"Yes," Donk said, looking at the general. "He's going to die."

General Mohammed frowned and spoke again. The man's face, Donk thought, was 70 percent nose. Hassan translated. "His doctor says there is one thing that can help him."

"What's that?" Donk asked, the second word cracking as it left his mouth. He was still looking at the general.

"There is a grass that grows in a valley in the mountains. A special grass. Medicine grass?"

"Medicinal grass."

"Yes. This grass his doctor can boil for Mister Graves, he says. Then Mister Graves can drink the broth." General Mohammed spoke again, nodded, and returned to his book. "He says Mister Graves will get better." Hassan shrugged.

"He has malaria," Donk told Hassan numbly. "Grass won't help malaria. He needs antibiotics." Donk had not meant for Hassan to translate this, but he did.

"Yes," General Mohammed said, through Hassan. As the general went on Hassan began to shift and nod. "Okay, now he says once he suffered this himself. Six years ago, in the summer?" General Mohammed kept talking. "And many of his men as well. They were all very ill, he says, just like Mister Graves. He says they have seen much of Mister Graves's sickness here. But they drank the boiled grass and a day later they were well."

"Do they have any of the grass here?"

"No. He says it is in a valley in the mountains beyond the village." Hassan listened. "He is saying now he can tell for you how to find the grass and give you two of his men. Together, he says, you can go get the grass. Then Mister Graves will be well." Hassan smiled.

"I need a vehicle," Donk said. He did not intend to find the grass. He would simply drive to Mazar. If General Mohammed's shadow-faced men did not care for this, they could shoot him. They could give Donk his own shadow face.

The general was reading again. When Hassan translated Donk's request, he breathed in deeply and turned a page. He spoke. Hassan: "It is not a far walk, he says. His men will show you."

"Tell him I need a vehicle."

General Mohammed peered at Donk over the top edge of his glasses and spoke, it was clear, for the last time. Hassan shook his head. "He says he is sorry, Mister Donk, but they have too many problems today to spare any vehicles to go to Mazar."

When Donk returned to Graves's room he found him asleep, his white face and reddish-purple cheeks agleam with perspiration, his forehead creased and dented. He was holding his purple Nokia. NO SIGNAL, its LCD read. Again Donk sat next to Graves's bed. Getting close to Graves was now like entering a force field of heat. He could smell Graves's bad breath, which smelled like shit, and his shit, which smelled like bad breath. Donk did not now believe and never had much believed in God or in human goodness. He did not think that people had a "time" they "had to go," or even that this special mountain grass would do fuck-all for Graves. He believed in and tried to think about very little. He believed in photography, which he loved, and death, which he hated. He thought about how he had been using one to deny the other. He thought about how clearly he felt death in Graves's bright room, the same greedy cool-edged core of heat that a decade ago he had felt zeroing in on his father. He refused to abandon Graves to it. Of course, this was just more ceremony. Graves was dying as he looked at him. But death, too, was ceremony, the one sacrament that, in time, singed every tongue.

Donk touched his own lips, absently. They were cold. No signal.

Hassan disagreed that helping Donk find medicinal grass was an implied part of his duties. He had no wish to leave the relative safety of this village. He seemed surprised, in fact, that Donk even wanted him along. Donk began to wonder if robbing them was not Hassan's polite if highly indirect way of attempting to end their association. The two soldiers General Mohammed lent Donk most clearly did not want to go find the grass either. The only person who wished less than they to go out and find this grass was Donk.

General Mohammed assured them that leaving by 1 p.m. would afford them plenty of time to find the valley, fill a satchel with grass, and return by evening. Before they left, one of General Mohammed's wives fed them all a pile of meatless pilau that they chased down with gallons of cherry compote.

Just outside the village, Donk watched as the two loaner soldiers loaded a small donkey with canvas pouches and plastic bags emblazoned with the Marlboro logo.

"Why," Donk asked Hassan, "are they bringing a goddamned donkey? We're only going to be gone for a few hours."

Hassan asked them, but the soldiers did not respond and kept loading the donkey with plastic bags. "I am thinking," Hassan hazarded, "that this donkey belongs to one of them. Like pet? Maybe they want it to receive its exercise today."

That these were not General Mohammed's ablest men was evident in several ways. They had been lucky enough to receive the American camouflage uniforms, but in place of the boots Donk saw on proud display among the general's other soldiers these men were wearing what he realized only incrementally were tire treads held to their feet by twine.

"I have a rule," Donk told Hassan to tell the soldiers, neither of whose names he had any interest in learning. "I'm going to call it Rule One. Rule One is: No talking. Unless it's an emergency, or unless they see the grass. Otherwise I don't want to hear any talking. Okay?"

Hassan looked troubled. "Mister Donk, why this rule?"

"Because I'm sick of talking, I'm sick of languages I don't understand, and I'm sick of words in general. I just want to walk."

"Can I talk if I talk English?"

Donk looked at him. "Did you steal my cameras?"

"Mister Donk! Why would I steal your cameras? Where would I put them?"

"You can talk in English. A little. But ask me first."

Hassan shook his head, lamely mouthed Donk's edict to the soldiers, then walked away a few feet and moped defeatedly. The soldiers had scarcely listened, their limited attention still fully commandeered by the donkey. The donkey was a youngish creature with a rust-and-toffee coat and teeth the size of shot glasses. Once it was loaded up, one of the soldiers smacked the donkey with proprietary cruelty on its bulbous muscular hindquarters. The donkey trundled forward a few steps, then stopped and shook its head, its long ears flapping. The first soldier, whose angular and almost handsome face was nearly hidden behind a bushy black beard that began growing just below his eyes, laughed. The second soldier, a smaller man whose beard was redder and less ambitious, walked over to the donkey and whipped it with a switch. This time the donkey walked and did not stop. Donk stared at the animal with dejected and secret confederacy, then followed after it.

They hiked for an hour without talking, saw no one, and reached the range's first serious hill just after two. They cleared it easily and, though another, steeper hill lay just ahead, Donk was pleased. These foothills were not very challenging. Even this range's highest faraway peaks were snowless. In Tajikistan he had trekked over far more punishing country. The trails were well worn and dusty, and the wind was low. The sun was bright; beneath it Afghanistan looked like a blizzard of gray and brown. A nature hike, minus the nature.

Donk thought back to the Porcupines in Upper Michigan, family trips his brother, Jason, now referred to as "hurt-feelings competitions." But Donk did not remember them this way. Donk was always deputized to carry the party's RV-sized tent, as well as anything that related to the inevitable screaming match that doubled as the tent's assembly. Donk had been a shortish, overweight boy, a puffing congenital sweater. On one trip, Jason had likened his younger brother's hunched appearance under thirty pounds of fatly wrapped weatherproofed nylon to that of a donkey. The word's homophonic closeness to Duncan or, worse, Dunc, his family nickname, did not immediately occur to Jason, and for the remainder of the trip Duncan inured himself to being known as "Donkey Boy." On their last night in the Porcupines—traditionally, the one time their father let the boys drink beer before they headed back to Milwaukee—Duncan had plunged his hand into their cooler's watery lukewarm dregs in search of a can of Miller Lite. "Hey, Donk," Jason called over, distracted with the fire. "Grab me one too?" Donk knew, even before Jason and his father had exchanged looks of revelation, that he had just been rechristened. The nickname spread as though it were a plot. His mother was the longest holdout, but after six months he was Donk even to her. He thought that nothing could have ever happened to him out there. That was what the trips now meant to him. They were pre-danger. Pre-death. Once, after he had had too much to drink during one of his infrequent visits back to the Midwest, Jason had unkindly disclosed that the trips' whole purpose had been their father's attempt to rid Donk of what the man always called "that goddamn baby fat." This had hurt Donk, a little.

"Mister Donk," Hassan said, apprehensive to be violating Rule One, "you are well?"

"Fine," Donk said. "Some dirt in my eye."

Hassan almost smiled. "Both eyes?"

Hassan was smarter than Donk realized. Everyone, Donk thought, was smarter than you realized. "Yes, Hassan. Both eyes."

Hassan fretted with the front flap of his *shalwar khameez*. "Mister Donk, I have maybe an emergency."

"Oh?"

"I think perhaps General Mohammed's soldiers are not pleased."

"What makes you say that?"

Hassan was quiet a moment, listening to the soldiers. They were ten feet back, softly chatting, their rifles' thin black straps cutting across their chests and their tire-tread sandals slapping against the hard soil. Their language sounded to Donk, strangely, like yodeling. Hassan edged closer to Donk and whispered, "They are talking about leaving us."

"Fuck them, then. I have a compass. I can find our way back. We don't need them."

"But what of the grass?"

Donk had completely forgotten about the grass.

"I am thinking," Hassan said, looking straight ahead, "that these are bad men."

The second hill took longer to climb. It was steeper, the path more friable. The sun's warmth had opened Donk's eyebrow, and sweat soaked into the wound lividly. The donkey, especially, was having trouble, its hard little hoofs slipping in the thick gray gravel. Red Beard decided the best way to hasten the donkey's ascent was to whip it across the face with his switch. The donkey hissed at him, its huge rotten teeth bared, its eyes rolling wildly in their sockets. Red Beard whipped it again, this time across the nose. Black Beard observed all this with nodding satisfaction. Hassan shook his head wretchedly, turned away, and kept walking. As the beating went on, it gathered a terrible energy, as crying does, as pain does, and Donk took a seat on a pathside stone and watched. As bad as he felt for the animal he was not about to step between it and Red Beard, whose streak of ferruginous cruelty was certain to run deeper than Donk could even begin to imagine. Thus he was cheered when the donkey, rearing bronco-style on its hind legs, its huge testicles bouncing, cunningly maneuvered its position in such a way as to deliver into Red Beard's chest a quick and astonishingly forceful double-barreled kick. Red Beard managed, somehow, to stay on his feet. After a few moments of absorption, however, his expression loosened, opening to a hundred new possibilities of pain. He dropped his stick and—gently—sat down. He rolled onto his side and rocked back and forth in the dirt. Donk noticed, remotely, that Red Beard was barefoot. The donkey had kicked him right out of his tire-tread sandals. With equal remoteness, Donk watched Black Beard calmly level his Kalashnikov at the donkey and squeeze off three quick rounds into its hindquarters. The donkey kicked blindly a few more times and then galumphed down the path, back toward the village, screaming. That was, Donk thought, really the only word for the sound he was now hearing: screaming. It did not get far. With the Kalashnikov's stock tucked snugly into his shoulder, Black Beard tracked the donkey and fired twice. The donkey's head kicked up, the reports' echoes saturating the afternoon air. The donkey staggered ahead for a few steps more, tried to turn around, then dropped onto its side. Its legs were still moving at different speeds and in different directions. In the meantime, Red Beard had struggled to his feet. With one arm wrapped around his cracked rib cage, he limped over to Donk and spoke.

Hassan was shaking with terror; his voice broke register as he translated. "Mister Donk, he says he is injured and requests that we go back."

Donk nodded at Red Beard thoughtfully, his hands tucked away in his hooded sweatshirt's front pockets to hide the fact that they were trembling. "Tell him, Hassan, that when we have the grass we can go back."

"He says he is injured very badly."

"Tell him this is his own stupid fucking fault."

"You tell him this!" Hassan cried.

Black Beard, his Kalashnikov now slung over his shoulder, was pulling the pouches and Marlboro bags off the donkey. Donk was about to speak when he noticed Black Beard stand quickly and look off warily to the east, instinctively reaching around for his rifle but not unshouldering it. Before Donk had even turned his head he heard the hollow patter of an approaching horse, then a low snorty sound. Upon the horse was a soldier. He rode in slowly, stopping at the midpoint between Donk and Black Beard, whose hand was still frozen in midreach for his rifle. The soldier looked to Donk, then to the dead donkey. Finally he rode over and circled the donkey's corpse, looking over at Black Beard only after he had made a complete orbit.

"Salaam," the soldier said, his horse's ears smoothed back, clear evidence of its distress at the sight of its murdered cousin.

"Salaam," Black Beard returned, his hand lowering.

The soldier was an American. His fatigues were lightly camouflaged, a few blobby splashes of faint green and wavy brown upon a dirty tan background. His backpack's two olive-green straps ran vertically down his chest. Another, thicker strap corseted his waist, and two more cinched around his thigh, where a 9mm pistol was sheathed in a camouflaged holster. Affixed upon his shoulder was the bulky black control pad for his air-to-ground radio, its CB hooked to his waist. Somewhat ostentatiously, Donk felt, he was wearing a floppy Afghan *pakul,* and around his neck was the same make of white scarf Donk had bought in Kunduz. He galloped over to Donk, young and triumphantly blue-eyed, his nose snout-like and his chin weak. A southerner, Donk guessed. Obviously he was one of the commandos Donk had only heard about, Special Forces boys leading on horseback whole garrisons of guerrillas, shining lasers into the nasties' mountain hidey-holes for the F/A-18s' laser-guided bombs, and vacuuming up customs and language as they went. Some of these guys, it was rumored, had been here as early as September 14.

It was against SF doctrine to travel alone, and Donk imagined that right about now he was zooming up in the digital viewfinder of the binoculars that belonged to this commando's partner, who was no doubt watching from a hill or was perhaps even hidden in some impossibly nearby rocks.

"Sir," the commando said to Donk. "You're an American?"

Donk pulled his hands from his sweatshirt's pockets and stood. "I am."

The commando, squinting, gazed down at Donk from his mount. He threw off the hard, unapproachable aura of sunlight on sheet metal. "Are you wounded?"

"What?"

The soldier tapped himself above the eye.

"No," Donk said, touching himself there and, with a flinch, regretting it. "It's nothing. A car accident."

"Sir, I've been following you. And I have to ask what you're doing out here, for one, and, for two, why are your men discharging their weapons in a hostile area?"

"They executed our donkey," Donk said. "I'm not sure why. And they're not my men. They're General Ismail Mohammed's."

The horse footed back a few steps, its huge stone-smooth muscles sliding around one another beneath a dark-brown coat as shiny as chocolate pudding. The commando, with the steadiness of a centaur, had not taken his eyes off Donk. "That leaves what you're doing out here."

"I'm a journalist. My friend is back in General Mohammed's village, like I said. He's very sick. I'm out here looking for grass."

The commando stared at him. "Pardon me, sir, but the stuff practically falls out of the trees here. There's no need to be out this—"

"Not marijuana. Grass. A special kind of grass."

"Ho-kay," he said.

"Look, forget that. Can you help me?"

"Sir, I don't really have any guidance."

"Any what?"

"Guidance, sir. I can't talk to the media."

Donk always admired military men, young military men in particular, for their peculiarly unsullied minds. "I'm not looking for an interview. My friend has malaria. He's back in General Mohammed's village. He's dying."

"Sir, be advised that these mountains are not safe for civilians. They're crawling with hostiles. And I don't mean to sound like a hard-ass, but I'm not really authorized to use this radio for anything other than ordering air strikes. We're doing pest control, sir, and I strongly recommend you get back to that village."

"Where's your commanding officer?"

"He's in Mazar-i-Sharif, sir."

"Lieutenant Marty, right?"

The commando paused. "I'm not at liberty to say, sir."

"Look, do you have any malaria medicine? Antibiotics? Anything you have. Believe me when I say it's an emergency."

The commando pulled back on the reins. The horse turned with the finicky heaviness particular to its species, and the commando started off.

Donk was not surprised. "This is all about reporters fucking you guys over in Vietnam, isn't it?" he called after him. "Well, you should know I was about six when Saigon fell. Were you even born?"

The commando stopped and turned back to him. "Leave this area, sir. Now."

Donk saluted the commando, who politely returned the salute and ya'd his horse to a full gallop. The cool thin dust swallowed them both just before they would have vanished over the nearest hill's lip. Donk asked Hassan to inform Black Beard and Red Beard that his mission was now under the protection of the American military, owners of fearsome fighter planes, magical horseback summoners of aerial bombs, benevolent providers of PX-surplus camouflage. Neither Red Beard nor Black Beard had much of anything to say after that.

Shortly after 4 p.m. they found the valley where the grass was supposed to grow, a large scooped-out gouge of grayish sand and brown rocky soil amid a ragged perimeter of half a dozen steep hills. A long twisty road wended through the valley and disappeared into an identically shady pass at each end. The hill they were now atop had provided them the least hospitable, most distinctly mountainous trek yet. Its top ridge was cold, windy, and dustless. As they stood in the sunlight looking down into the valley, Donk saw why the commando had wanted him to return to General Mohammed's village. Along the valley's road was a smudged line of charcoal-colored transport trucks and pickups. Black Beard withdrew from one of his satchels a pair of binoculars. After having a look he handed the binoculars without comment to Donk. They were, Donk saw, cheap enough to have been pulled from a cereal box. Nonetheless, they helped him discern that the smudges were blast marks; the dark charcoal color could be credited to the fact that each vehicle had been incinerated from the outside in. It took them another twenty minutes to climb down into the valley, and they walked along the road's wreckage as warily and silently as animals. The bombing had not happened terribly recently. Not a single piece of hardware was smoking, and the truck husks had the brittle, crumbly look of a scorched old log one cleared from a well-trafficked campsite's pit before building a new fire. The wreckage looked picked over, and the shrapnel was in careful little piles. Black Beard and Red Beard muttered to themselves.

"What are they saying?" Donk asked Hassan.

Hassan shook his head. "Their prayers for the dead."

"But these men were their enemies."

"Of course," Hassan said, looking at Donk hatefully.

Donk approached the bombed convoy's lead vehicle. Its tires had melted and its doors were gone. The empty cab and bed were both largely intact, though they had been parted from each other after sustaining what looked like a direct hit. There were no craters, Donk knew, because this campaign's bombs were designed to explode a few feet above their targets. Donk walked farther down the blasted line. He did not see any bodies at all until the penultimate vehicle, a nearly vaporized Datsun pickup so skeletal it looked like a blackened blueprint of a Datsun pickup. The charred driver was barely distinguishable from the wreckage around him. He was just a crispy torso of shrunken unrealness. His face and hair had been burned off, his head a featureless black oval. Donk reached for the camera he did not have and stepped closer, discovering that the reason no one had moved his body was because it was melted to its seat. His stomach gurgled and turned. Something in him clenched. He did not have his camera. The image would never swim up at him from the bottom of a plastic platter filled with developing fluid. It would stay exactly this way. . . . Donk forced the thought away.

"Mister Donk!" Hassan called.

He turned, rubbing his beating heart through his chest. "Yes, Hassan. What is it?"

He pointed at the Beards. "They say the grass is nearby."

Donk took in this information. He felt the same mild surprise he remembered experiencing when he had learned, thanks to a concert Tina had taken him to, that people were still writing symphonic music. Surprise that he would be so surprised. The grass actually existed. How unaccountable. "Where?"

Hassan pointed across the valley. "They say over there."

Donk looked. At the far side of the valley stood a sparse stand of trees, the first trees he had seen all day. They made him feel better, somehow. Around the trees was a long squarish field of desiccated grass the color of wheat. The road this annihilated convoy had been traveling along would have taken them right past that field. They walked, Black Beard and Red Beard having now unshouldered their weapons. Walking across this valley felt to Donk like standing in the middle of an abandoned coliseum. Above, the sky was getting darker. The day was silent. Donk noticed, as they grew closer to the trees, that they had not yet completely shed their leaves, little pompoms of bright orange and yellow still tipping their branches. The setting sun was pulling a long curtained shadow across this valley. He realized, then, that even if they pushed themselves they were not going to make it back to the village before nightfall. He hurried himself ahead, and Hassan and the Beards jogged to keep pace with him. He did not care to learn who or what ruled these hills at night.

"Mister Donk," Hassan said, "please slow!"

"Fuck off," he called back. Donk's thoughts suddenly felt to him alien and disfigured, exalted by fear, disconnected from the internal key that transformed them into language. He veered off the road and sprinted toward the trees through grass abruptly growing all around him. His boots were scything up great cheerful swaths of the stuff. He did not know why he was not gathering up any of it. He was not certain what might make one kind of grass more restorative than another. He had a quiet, appalled thought at all the things he did not know. He then remembered to believe that the grass was not going to help Graves. Not at all.

"Mister Donk!" Hassan called again. Donk turned to see Hassan following him across the field of grass in an unsteady, not-quite-running way. "They say we must be careful here! Mister *Donk*!" Black Beard, now shouting something himself, endured a moment of visible decision making, then left the road and followed after Hassan.

Donk's head swiveled forward. He was almost to the trees. The grass just under the trees looked especially boilable, thick and tussocky. Then, oddly, Donk seemed to be looking at the trees and the grass from much higher up. His horizon lifted, then turned over. Donk had heard nothing, but when he landed he smelled something like cooked meat, cordite, loam. He lay there in the grass, blinking. With his fingers he pulled up a thick handful of grass, then let it go. He looked over. Hassan was beside him, ten feet away, screaming, though still Donk could hear nothing. Hassan's mouth was bloody and his cardigan sweater was gone but for some shreds, and what Donk initially believed to be large fat red leeches were crawling all over his stomach and chest. On the other side of him Black Beard was creeping away on all fours, shaking his head in a dazed way. After a few feet he stopped and lay down. Donk thought that he, Donk, was okay. But for some reason he could not sit up. His legs felt funny, as did his back. He did not panic and lifted his left leg to watch the tendons and veins and muscles fall away from it as though it were a piece of chicken that had been boiled too long. Then he was bleeding. The blood did not come out of him in a glug but in a steady silent gush. There was so much of it. He lowered his leg and from his prone position saw broken-ribbed Red Beard struggling down the road. Yes, he thought, that's right. Go get help. Donk thought he was going to be all right. It did not hurt yet. Oh wait yes it did. Suddenly it hurt very, very much. Donk always believed that you learned a lot about a place by the first thing you heard said there. In Chechnya it was "It doesn't work." In Rwanda: "I don't know." In Afghanistan: "Why are you here?" He had not stepped on a mine. Slowly, he knew that. No reason to waste an expensive mine in such a remote place. He had stepped instead on a bomblet, a small and festively yellow cluster of ordnance that had not detonated above the eradicated convoy but rather bounced away free and clear and landed here in the grass. Hassan was no longer screaming but simply lying there and looking up at the sky. He, too, was mechanically blinking. Hassan needed help. Donk did not care if he stole his cameras. Donk could help him. Donk, suddenly, loved him. But first he had to rest. He could not think about all this until he had some fucking rest. Could he get some rest? He had to help Graves because if he did not Graves would die. He thought of his father, how he had looked in the end. God, Donk thought, I do not want to die. But he did not much care for old age either. A problem there. "Dad!" Donk yelled out suddenly. He did not know why; something in him unclenched. Or maybe he had not said anything at all. It was hard to tell, and it was getting dark. So: rest. Rest here one minute and off we go. Red Beard could use the company. Use the help. Ho-kay. He was all right. He just needed to figure this out.

Aral

P lease," he said to the American, blowing into his teacup with a delicacy that did not suit him, "you must eat more."

"No," the American said in mild return. "Thank you." She was exhausted. They'd been speaking for nearly three hours, and though she was famished—she hadn't eaten all day—the notion of food or, more precisely, *his* food made her stomach knot. Self-righteousness, this was—stupidity—but she refused to let him spelunk his way into any of her weaknesses. He smiled at the American's refusal; then, with both hands, he raised the teacup chin level and treated her to the theater of his blow-sip-blow method of tea intake.

The American's gaze slipped off him and again absorbed the room. It was resplendent, breathtaking: polychromatic tapestries on the wall, servile attendants stalking stiffly in and out, a low table scattered with more food, fruit, teapots, and silverware than seemed appropriate. They sat across from each other, on the floor, cross-legged, atop heavy blankets. She was unused to such long-term contortion and her feet had surpassed being merely asleep. They felt gone, disappeared, off in some other dimension. Part of the reason she no longer cared how long they sat here was that she had no idea how she would stand when they were finished.

Suddenly the man spoke to the attendants standing guard near the door in his native tongue, Uzbek, something the American did not understand (to her he spoke Russian). In a blink the table was cleared and the attendants were gone. They were alone. The instant the table was empty she wished she'd eaten something. Hunger stumbled, heavy-footed, inside her stomach.

"When will I get my passport?" the American asked, also in Russian, with a kind of graceless start-and-stop inflection.

"I'm not sure," the man said, deftly unfolding his legs and then refolding them.

"When will I be able to leave?"

"Of that too," he said, "I am unsure."

Her hands clenched. "All you have to do is call the United Nations. It's so—it's simple. *Call* them, *ask* them who I am."

The man said nothing for several moments, then *tsk*ed once, impassively. The American pulled herself together and saw that in the meantime he'd made a small pointed pile of bread crumbs on the tablecloth with his knife. "To be a woman," he said with disinterest, tending to his pile, "and to travel alone—this is unwise in our nation."

It was interesting to her how little the man's sexism bothered her now, how secondary such concerns had become. "I told you what happened. My colleagues are in Tashkent. They were ill. I speak the language; I was anxious; I didn't feel like waiting for them, and—"

"And off you went," he said, smiling, "to our Aral Sea." Her gaze collapsed when confronted with his smile. He was missing at least a dozen teeth, the replacements either gold or some shiny alchemic substitute, and his remaining teeth looked like a museum of cavities. Other than this distraction, he was not a bad-looking man. His hair was short, bristly, black, spangled by dandruff. His equally black mustache fell only a little short of achieving Fu Manchu proportions. His neck was too thin compared to the rest of his body; he reminded her of a saber or a long fish, a northern pike or a gar—something sharp, severe.

"I've told you," she said. "I'm a biologist. I was sent by the UN to—"

"I know who you are," he cut in, with fresh displeasure, "and I know who sent you."

She was astonished. It was the first time he'd spoken to her as if he believed she was who she claimed to be. He sat there, pleased with her struck-dumbness, and she realized with something like complete certainty that he'd always believed she was who she said she was; he *knew* it. The dynamic of their relationship changed so swiftly the American imagined she felt a breeze slide over her.

"You," he said, "are Amanda Reese. You are an American. You work with the United Nations." He found no consolation, she could tell, from telling her the truth. He gained no clearheaded frankness, no serendipitous nobility. "You are a biologist from the University of Indiana."

"Illinois," she said quietly.

He smirked. "Excuse me. Illinois." He pronounced it Russian-style, *E-lee-NOIS*, though she had not. She felt oddly lifted by this, superior.

"I think you know my next question," she said. But the language tripped her up. Finding the words was getting more difficult as she grew more exhausted. She felt as if she were digging around in a darkened attic for something she knew only by sight, and she hoped he'd missed her grammatical mistake.

He hadn't. He held up a finger and repeated her sentence, gently correcting her Russian, something about the correct adjective ending. His raised finger did not retreat until she said it again, correctly.

"High school was a long time ago," she mumbled in excuse. But she'd also studied in college, after college, before coming; she'd studied more than she would have admitted to anyone. Still, despite the huge vocabulary that years of studying had harvested, she was terrible, stump-tongued, a syntax butcher. "No gift" was how her most patient tutor, Vova Petrovich, had once sadly appraised her. *No geeft, Amanda, you hev no geeft.*

"I understand," he said in English. His head tipped forward adroitly on his thin neck. "School was long ago for me too." In Russian: "Your question, yes? When will you leave? Professor Reese," he said, leaning back, "you may leave whenever you want. You are not imprisoned. On the contrary, you are my guest."

"I'm not leaving until I get my passport—and until I can tell the UN about my treatment here."

Now he laughed, his eyes doubling in size. "Your *treatment*!" This burst out of him. He looked around for someone to join this ebullience, found no one, and stopped laughing as suddenly as he had begun. "Yes, your treatment is something I'd like to discuss as well, Professor Reese. From the airport you were chauffeured here"— he motioned around him, underscoring the room's bright opulence—"and offered lunch, which, I might add, you refused." He smiled again. "Yes, let us tell the United Nations how you were treated, Professor Reese."

"I know who you are," she said.

He looked at her with distaste. "Of that," he said, "I have my doubts."

"Kah Gay Bay," she said quickly. KGB. He raised his eyebrows in polite acknowledgment, obviously pleased the initials carried such mythic tonnage in her mind's canals. "That's who you are. And I know what you do."

He ran his index fingers along the gutters under his eyes, clearing away the silt.

"Get me my passport," she said. "Right now, god-dammit."

He said nothing, again treating her to his freighted, sullen silence. "I will not keep you any longer, Professor Reese," he said at last. "But I would like to hear your UN's thoughts about our problem before you go."

She regarded him coldly. "*Our* problem?"

For once, this man seemed honest in his surprise. "Why, Professor Reese," he said. "I speak of the Aral Sea, of course."

She was an environmental biologist, though she would have resented being pinned to merely one biological discipline, since like most biologists she had several realms of interest and thought herself bright about many things. Her specialty was irrigation: its almost incomprehensibly far-ranging effects both on the irrigated area and on the area whose irrigation was diverted. She was in fact held to be one of America's most accurate prognosticators on the often unpredictable and occasionally ecocidal effects of the always ill-advised practice of monkeying with rivers, lakes, and seas. She was a recent and uncommonly young recipient of tenure, author of dozens of articles, coeditor of a cobbled-together collection of essays whose slant grew before her eyes to be so idiotically anti-industry its existence embarrassed her to this day. She was "famous in certain circles," as she often heard her mother say to guests when she thought her daughter out of earshot, during those long July days she spent summering with her parents in Vermont. "Our little Rachel Carson." But this dotage was embarrassing, and ridiculous besides: Who *isn't* famous in "certain circles"? Although of course it was her desire to garner true, unqualified Rachel Carson fame that disqualified what most people would have accepted as God's plenty.

Initially, she studied biology to work in the sea (which she had yet to do); her pursuit of the stumbling, bearlike Russian language had its germ in a bizarre teenage infatuation with chess (indirectly) and Boris Spassky (directly);

she had never married though had once been close, which is how she'd become involved with the United Nations' Aral Sea Basin Relief Project one year ago. Getting a government job—a job with any government, she was confident—had less to do with personal excellence than did a professional wrestling match, and though Amanda was no hardened cynic she accepted this more or less uncritically, just as she had uncritically accepted the job with the Aral project that her former lover, Andrew, had more or less gift-wrapped for her.

Once upon a time, the name *Aral Sea* was accurate. Since 1960, however—when Soviet engineers began to divert its twin tributaries to fertilize cotton fields in Turkistan—the Aral had gone from a sea of plenty to a sea of less plenty, to an unfortunate polluted lake, to a poison lake to a shrinking pestilent bog to a certified disaster. That was where it stood when Amanda was named part of a ten-scientist team acting as a stateside academic/scientific codicil to an Aral Sea Basin Relief Project—no longer the Aral Sea at all but the Aral Disaster.

Of course, she had never actually expected to get to *see* the Aral Sea. Mostly she crunched numbers, calculating the average increase of temperature and decrease of airborne moisture and what that would mean, hypothetically, for the surrounding area's agriculture. She ran computer simulations that posited what would happen with no Aral Sea at all. She e-mailed her findings to other biologists and tried to forget about the decades of pollution and insecticide and toxins in the Aral's exposed and windblown seabed. She also tried to forget that the sanitized, bloodless, glowing-green numbers on her Hewlett-Packard's screen told her seventeen thousand kids who in nearly any other part of the world would have been learning multiplication tables and team sports were going to be anemic.

Her alpha-and-omega trip to the Soviet Union had been to Moscow, in 1987, as Andrew's guest (he was then working for the ambassador), and she'd bathed in the springy feeling of glasnost. What she saw was not the nation of wicked Lenin, evil Stalin, warty Brezhnev, but Pepsi billboards and gleaming hotels and elegant, jaw-dropping cocktail parties. This was her week in Russia, and she had spoken the language twice (*"Skazhite, pozhaluista, gde tualet?"* and *"Taksi!"*).

Of course, everything was different now. For one, Andrew was gone. Aral was worse. The Soviet Union was no more. Along with the tourist-perfect, industry-friendly teardrop-and-puddle nations that had sprouted along Russia's western flank, a jigsaw of polysyllabic, hostile-sounding nations had metastasized to the south. Central Asia, this was, and the Aral Sea was its fountain of life.

When Amanda learned that, thanks to her Russian skills, her days of computer simulations and guesswork were over—she was *going* there, as in *next month,* with two other members of the team to survey the Aral Sea basin personally—she called up her old tutor, Vova, and asked him what was Central Asia's story anyway? Vova said, "Theenk of Ziberia, Amanda, fleeped over." Had he ever been there, seen it? "Amanda, Amanda," he said, becoming serious, nearly bitter, his accent suddenly falling away.

"The only Russians in Central Asia are the ones whose relatives were exiled there." She sensed him shaking his head at the boundless naïveté Americans had for places that weren't America. "Don't you think they knew what they were doing when they decided to murder the place?"

She learned more about Central Asia on the plane while gliding over the Ukraine from Ted Whitford, PhD, Marine Biology, UCLA. He too spoke some Russian (he'd spent time in Murmansk while studying the Barents Sea), and they practiced together until he realized she knew more than he did and put a stop to it right then and there. An asshole, Ted was. But he seemed to know a lot about the Aral Sea. (A disarmingly accurate generalization about assholes: They all know a lot, however brittle their knowledge becomes under intimacy's whitest, hottest lights.) What he told her was specific, real-seeming—more information, at least, than the UN's ossifyingly dull dossiers were willing to provide. Ted Whitford mentioned cities and local nationals he'd spoken to, supplying bleak sketches of how annihilated the Aral's fishermen had been. He spoke with the world-weariness of one who simply knows too much. Had he been to Uzbekistan, the country that bore the brunt of Aral's ailments? Amanda asked. Once, Ted explained, to Tashkent, the capital, which was still pretty Russian. More Russian than Russia, in fact. Ha-ha.

On her own, Amanda had learned that the rest of the world had, by and large, dismissed Central Asia and its problems with Aral; that most of the solutions for the problem cost somewhere in the twelve-figure range; that the UN was trying to do everything it could, but until Central Asia's nations began to cooperate on water allocation and set prices for water usage like the good little budding market-economy nations they claimed they wanted to be, there was little the UN could do. Add to this the fact that the Aral Sea was found in one of Uzbekistan's biggest headaches, Karakalpakistan, a nominally sovereign republic with its own government, bureaucracy, and eddies of red tape apart from Uzbekistan's, and you were left navigating waters too tricky even for the United Nations. The entire scenario had the fiendish unsolvability of a physics story problem, and Amanda felt both intimidated and relieved. She and her team couldn't, even at their least effective, possibly make anything worse.

"It's damn sad," Ted Whitford concluded with a sigh. "It rips me up. *Damn* sad."

"Sounds like it," said Michael Nam, sitting across the aisle from Amanda and Ted, reading the Cadogan guide to Central Asia (Amanda had *Lonely Planet*). Amanda had sat next to Michael on the first leg of the trip, over the Atlantic. She leaned forward to wink at him, become an accomplice to his insult of Ted in some way, but he did not look over at her. Instead, he turned the page in his book and pushed his styleless, thick-lensed glasses farther up his bridge. Michael was Korean, from the University of Miami—the "Carl Sagan of oceanography," as she'd once heard him described. From their earlier conversation,

Amanda had concluded that he, too, was an asshole, but an abidable, even interesting asshole.

"Righto," Ted said to Michael and, alarmingly, touched Amanda on the knee.

"How long before we reach Tashkent?" Amanda asked Michael, again leaning forward.

"Two hours," Michael said, closing his book and then his eyes.

Amanda looked around the plane. Nearly everyone was asleep, one or two souls glowing like angels under their reading lights. As far as she could tell, she and her colleagues were the only Americans on board. Her around-the-world trip was in its twentieth hour, and she was wide awake. She closed her eyes anyway, but opened them when Ted once again began talking. She turned to him and saw he'd not been speaking to her. He was addressing a small handheld tape recorder, whispering intense Churchillian cadences into it: "I'd say we're at thirty-five thousand feet," he was saying. Amanda rolled her head as far away from him as physiology would permit. "Tashkent," he said, milking it, "Tash*kent* is down there too." A pause of several moments. "And so is Aral. It all makes Murmansk and Barents . . . *Jesus!* Kid stuff, Ted. It was kid stuff."

While they waited in the customs line, Amanda first began to grow nervous. She could see quite a bit of the airport behind the customs booth but no one was there, not a soul. She tapped Michael, who was still reading his travel guide, on the shoulder. "Hey. Who's supposed to meet us here, anyway?"

Michael frowned and dug into his breast pocket. "Some guy named Nuridinov, from the Ministry of Water, and two other gentlemen. I can't seem to read this." He frown-squinted. "Hm. My own damn handwriting, too."

"I don't see *anyone*, Michael," Amanda said. The customs line opposite hers was for nationals, and every dark-skinned, black-headed, heavy-lidded man in that line stood facing her, staring. She was, it dawned on her, the only woman in the entire terminal. She thought herself an attractive woman, though not anyone an American male would cross the street for. But in the present situation she might as well have been a movie star, despite her no-nonsense shoulder-length auburn hair and her breast-less, mousy trimness. (She was trim in the absurd, magical way only women with large rear ends and thick thighs can be, these last two something not even five days of lap swimming a week could dragon-slay.) She found herself longing for the Slavic familiarity of Moscow and stared at the clipped black hairs on the back of Michael's neck. Ted was behind her, still recording: "Our line is not moving. . . . Some locals appear to be staring at me. . . ."

"Someone's waiting," Michael said, after looking up at the empty terminal himself. Amanda nodded uneasily.

They got through customs, got their luggage, and planted themselves near the airport's main entrance. No one was there. No one came. Three times Amanda had to explain to curious, walking-by *militsiya* who they were, why they were waiting. By 7 a.m. they were told to move along. Michael was in charge of this little field trip, but he'd never been given any phone numbers. It had been assumed they wouldn't need any. Someone would meet them. Amanda and Michael were outside the airport in the pinkish, dirty light, discussing whether to call the American embassy or go to their hotel, when Ted appeared with what he optimistically called break-fast. It was some rancid-smelling meat wrapped up in a pitalike pocket and smothered with onions. Shashlik, Ted called it. "Here. I had it when I was here before. It's delicious."

"No, thanks," Amanda said. "I don't eat anything off the street."

"It's not off the street," Ted said, and pointed. "It's from him." A small mustached man waved from behind the shashlik stand fifty yards away. They all waved back, idiotically.

Michael took the shashlik from Ted and absently tore into it, tracing his finger across the map of Tashkent in his guidebook. "Look," he said. "I say we get to the hotel. They're probably waiting for us there anyway. Change of plans. Something."

Amanda stepped back; she'd let them decide. She was happy so far only to be here, to see what those numbers became when made flesh and blood. She'd see it for better or for worse and was prepared, she thought, for either. Tashkent was beginning to stir. Car horns sounded off far away; the morning was already growing hot, smog saturating the air. She sucked in sharply and with crossed eyes coughed out her intake. She'd taken hits off hash pipes less potent than Tashkent's morning air.

When she rejoined Ted and Michael, it appeared they'd settled on the hotel, no doubt deeming it too embarrassing to go running off to the embassy just yet for help. They accepted her back into the huddle with a nod and told her what they were doing, making no pretense that her vote even mattered. *Honest, at least*, she thought.

"Standing up the United Nations," Ted said, amused, polishing off his shashlik. "Now I've truly seen it all."

***

"Explain to me," the American said, "how Aral can possibly be *our* problem when you people make it impossible for us to help you."

"How quickly you boil us down to one homogeneous people, Professor Reese. I am one man. How do I make it impossible for you to help us?"

"I'm speaking in generalities."

"Ah."

"I've read briefings. People here think nothing of letting their spigots run all day. That's why our primary advice is that you start charging your citizens for water usage."

"The Aral Sea is dead, Professor. Charging families who cannot afford it will not bring it back to life. You scold us like we are children. Americans enjoy this, it seems."

"We just enjoy paranoid totalitarian regimes forced to

tell the truth for once and admit their monstrosities, that's all."

"Blind children, Professor, have no stake in any regime. Nor do anemic pensioners."

"It's obvious we view this problem differently. But there are—"

"The difference between us, Professor, is that we know what suffering is. I know more about you—the many soft American indulgences—than you can hope to know of yourself. I know of your businessmen who fuck our women like cheap whores, your corporations that take advantage of our workers while thinking we are too stupid to know the difference, your Peace Corps workers who castigate us as lazy and stinking. You have no tragedy and forget that such things exist, and if you know they do, you blame those whom the tragedy befalls. Americans are a people who've let their souls grow fat."

"Then why even bother doing anything, if you're so proud of suffering? Let it and everyone die. So, we've talked. Now let me go. I don't even know where I am, where my companions are."

"Mr. Whitford and Mr. Nam are at the American embassy, Professor Reese, presently searching for you. It is, in fact, something of a crisis."

"What? How do you know that?"

"..."

"*How* do you know that?"

"We are the KGB. I know this as I knew you were coming here, as I knew whom you were to meet at the airport."

"Nuridinov—"

"An easier man to bribe than I thought possible, even by our standards."

"Wait a minute. . . . *Bribe?*"

"Certainly. How else would I guarantee his not joining you at the airport?"

"You *planned* all this?"

"I tried, Professor. Alas, everything has gone wrong. This, too, is common for our people. Now, come, we must stand."

"Why are—what are you talking about?"

"We are going, Professor."

"Going where? I'm not going anywhere with you. Get the American embassy on the phone right now."

"Americans rely too much on this device, I think. You don't need it. Professor Reese, I'm taking you to the very place you traveled seventeen thousand kilometers to see."

"Aral? It's close?"

"From my heart, Professor, the Aral Sea is never far."

———

A note had greeted them at the hotel check-in desk. Amanda handed it to Michael, who unshouldered his luggage onto the polished floor and murmured its text incredulously: "'Forgive us, kind gentlemen, but we are forced to meet you in Nukus, tomorrow. Things have risen.'" Softly Michael repeated the last line over again—*things have risen*—then flipped the paper over as if searching for the elliptical message's tail. "It's not even signed," he said. But stapled to the note were three plane tickets for tomorrow's flight to Nukus, on the western side of the country.

Ted was chewing on his pipestem, leaning against the check-in desk, buried to midthigh in sporty Day-Glo luggage. "Oh, hell, Michael," he confided, giving him a manly swat on the back, "welcome to the former Soviet Union. Nothing ever works. Don't sweat it. It used to take me a week in Murmansk just to place an overseas phone call."

Michael was simmering like a spanked child, staring at the plane tickets helplessly. When the words registered, he turned to Ted with an apoplectic slackness to his face. "Well, this *isn't* Murmansk, Ted, in case you *hadn't* noticed"—he was, incredibly, hissing—"and we're *not* here to study *brine* in the North *Atlantic*; we're *here* with the fucking United *Nations* and I'm *sorry* if it's just too fucking *much* on my part to *expect* someone to *be* here!"

While Ted quietly, indignantly, returned fire, Amanda interrupted the drowsing babushka behind the desk and booked two rooms.

The hotel was a middle-range affair, the lobby done up in a marblish, neo–*From Russia with Love* motif a clever film student might have thought touching. It was not the nicest hotel in Tashkent, nor was it the worst. The service industry here was still in its australopithecine stage, and the nicest hotels thought nothing of charging three hundred dollars a night for Best Western–quality rooms, a price the UN was simply unwilling to pony up for such a nonevent. That each member of their team had been given the Aral Relief project entirely on nepotistic grounds was well known, making them markedly easier to abuse.

Amanda had her own room, and as she double-checked the steadfastness of her small golden luggage locks she heard Ted and Michael next door, continuing their stilted lockjaw bickering. The narcotic fusion of jet lag and finally being alone knocked her out before she quite knew what was happening. She remembered only to set her alarm for the next morning.

She dreamed of seas and of Andrew, of drifting Cyrillic letters and of Connery's James Bond, and awoke at 5 a.m. to the sound of vomiting next door.

"I'm dying," Michael said, when he opened the door for her.

Amanda stepped in, hearing through the bathroom door the muffled, gastric trauma of Ted's stomach contents rapidly leaving his body, though from which exit she didn't know. Instinctively, her hand shot up to lie flush on Michael's forehead. It was hotter than a sauna rock. "Michael," she said.

They sat on the bed, Michael shivering as she put her arm around him. "The shashlik," he said, and smiled. His gentle Korean eyes, though, were wreathed with fear. "I'm fairly sure it's just food poisoning. You wait it out, you live through it, it goes away. I think I had something like this in Osaka once. We ported there while tracking whales, and I ate some sushi I shouldn't have. Familiarity's of slight consolation right now, I'm afraid."

Seeing him sick unhardened her heart toward him,

and she was moved by this attempt at bravery. He was making up, she knew, for his slippage in the lobby earlier. Amanda's forehead met his with a small suctionless thud. "Michael, I told you not to eat that thing." She smiled and shook her head.

Michael nodded, shivering more violently now. And suddenly the Carl Sagan of oceanography began to weep, sobbing and shuddering, though whether from pain, or hopelessness, or embarrassment, or fear of being sick in such a place, or the guilty futility one feels in countries less fortunate than America, she didn't know. She pulled the sheet from his bed and draped it over his shoulders and held him until Ted emerged, whiter than an igloo, from the bathroom.

"I've got the Dresden of diarrhea," he announced, wearing only a flimsy towel and propping himself up against the peeling hotel-room wall. His face was half shaven, as if he'd been preparing for his day when struck down by the thirsty protozoan horde swirling through his GI tract. "This is the Mother of all Diarrhea, people."

"I'm calling the embassy," Amanda said. Neither of them argued. The phone in their room did not work. The phone in her room did, but she was informed by the operator downstairs—an excitement blooming in her voice when she placed Amanda's accent and learned of her call's destination—that an outgoing call would be twenty-five American dollars, payable in advance at the front desk. "I've got to walk over there," Amanda told them when she came back. "Calling out from here's a pipe dream."

Both Ted and Michael were now in their slender single beds, their restless legs scissoring under the sheets and their hands plastered to their faces, as if trying to cool the burning brain pans behind their skulls. The room's intestinal stench was eye-watering.

"Amanda," Michael said, "listen." She looked at the empty travel bottles of Pepto-Bismol on the night table and at Ted, reaching over the edge of his bed and, without looking, digging in his carry-on. "We're going to wait this out. We talked about it. We can wait this out."

She brushed hair from her face. "Michael, let me call them at least—"

"We're waiting it out, Amanda. You go to Nukus and meet Nuridinov, and we'll be along in the next day or two. The flight leaves in two hours. If you want to catch it you've got to hurry."

"There's no reason to involve the embassy in this, Mandy," Ted said.

"This isn't a pissing contest, gentlemen. You're both ill, and we have no idea how seriously. Jesus, think about it! This is a no-brainer. Doesn't the embassy have a staff specifically for in-country nationals' emergencies?"

Ted spoke through his teeth. "I traveled through Commie Russia for six months, Amanda, and I never once so much as darkened the embassy's door. I'll be damned if I do it now."

Amanda, disgusted, merely stared at them, listening to the smooth fabric hiss of the beds' cheap material as her teammates writhed against it. After a while she said, "You're academics, you know, not superheroes."

Michael propped himself up to look at her. "If you

don't want to go alone, Amanda, we understand, but someone needs to call the ministry to tell them what's happened."

"Oh, for . . . I've got *no* problems with going alone, Michael. I speak Russian better than either one of you." She was about to explain that the only thing keeping her here was her concern for their well-being when a possibly delirious Ted stepped in:

"Then what's the fucking problem, you dumb cunt? Go."

She left.

—⁓—

"What's with the blindfold?" the American asked.

His response was two beats delayed; she'd interrupted him from something. "To make you sightless."

"*Other* than that," she said darkly.

"You will know soon. Do not be frightened."

"I'm too tired to be frightened," the American said. They had left Nukus's KGB building and were driven by her captor's chauffeur—the man who at the airport assured her he was from the Ministry of Water—to the city of Moynaq, a drive of two hours. Moynaq, like most of Uzbekistan's penumbral cities, was ornamented by nuclear-winter lassitude, but due to its closeness to Aral it was worse off than most. Driving through its devastated streets felt to the American like putting on dirty clothes. In the middle of Moynaq they entered a run-down warehouse strewn with broken concrete and automobile shells; there her hands were bound and she was blind-folded, then put into another car—something bouncy like a dune buggy—where she sat alone for forty minutes until joined by her captor and three others. One was the driver, she knew. The other two were a mystery. She heard only their endless maneuvering against the back-torturing plastic seats and their steady breathing.

"Where are we going?" she asked, shouting over the insectoid drone of the engine. The dune buggy heaved and revved, the driver swearing heroically after more alarming bumps.

"I told you," the man said.

After an unidentifiable length of time, the dune buggy came to an inglorious, wheezing stop. She heard the driver light a cigarette. The mysterious passengers sighed quietly. Somewhere far away tractors were plowing. The wind pushed at her, the dust weaved into its invisible fabric whistling. Her head came to rest against the roll bar.

"Are you going to kill me?" the American asked, startled at how unmoved she was by this possibility.

The man exhaled sharply and laughed a little. "No, Professor Reese."

The American swiveled her head around. "It's bright."

"We are outside."

The American laughed herself now, then nodded. "You knew," she began, "that I was coming on that flight to Nukus alone. Right at the airport you knew to grab me."

"We had no idea you would be alone, Professor," he said. "Not at all. We thought all along professors Whitford and Nam would be with you."

"So the plan was to nab all of us."

"*Nab* is a sinister word, Professor. *Escort you* is perhaps more accurate."

"Why? Why is the government doing this when they're the ones who invited us here?"

He said nothing for a few moments and then cleared his throat. The two unknown passengers climbed out of the dune buggy and padded away on what sounded like gravel. When they were gone he told her, "My government, Professor, is unaware of what is happening here." And with a polite, regal-sounding "Excuse me," he left the vehicle as well.

The American sat there alone under the murderous sun, salted by the wind. She dozed for what might have been ten minutes or two hours and was awakened by rough sausagy fingers undoing her binds. *"Ket,"* the driver said to her when she was free. *"Khozer, tez-tez."*

"Ya ne govoryu po-uzbekski," the American told him. I don't speak Uzbek.

"Go," he said to her in Russian, and as she stood he peeled off her blindfold.

The sun nearly exploded her eyeballs. With a hopeful foot she tried to step out of the buggy and onto the running board but miscalculated. She smacked her lip against the roll bar as she tumbled out of the buggy and onto the ground. Her tongue probed the split lip. It had burst open like a ripe tomato. Cathedral bells gonged whole dirges in her head; salty, sulfurous dust filled her mouth. Dizzily she stood and looked around, her pupils mad, convulsing black pinpricks.

"It is unenjoyable," she heard behind her. She turned. There the man stood, a small well-dressed black-haired child on each side of him. His hands were on their backs and they stared at the space above the American's head with the emotion of rag dolls. Behind them were a half-dozen grounded, rusted-out fishing boats—a naval graveyard. Above the boats the sun sizzled like a cancerous boil in the yellow sky. She knew she was standing on what used to be the Aral Sea's silty floor. Once water had washed over the rocks beneath her feet, flickered against the ships' crumbling hulls, carried on its wave crests the burden of every creature's life for miles around her. It was a burden now lifted; she couldn't see anything for miles other than the graveyard's hulking tombstones and yellow-brown scree. She felt hotter right now than she imagined possible and fought back the urge to dry-heave, to faint.

From her split lip a thread of blood unspooled, stopping on the swell of her chin. She mopped it away with her pocket handkerchief and said, "What's unenjoyable?"

"Blindness," he said, and moved his hands from his children's backs to the tops of their heads. "Blindness," he said again, and looked away.

After a moment of puzzlement, the American caught the milkiness to the children's eyes, the unseeing patina coating their corneas. "Oh, Christ," she said, sighing it, and looked away herself.

"I thought the world would hear of this," the man said, still looking away from her, "if I showed the Americans." His smile became impish, then mischievous, so mischievous it took her a moment to recognize that he

86

was weeping. The children, under their father's hands, remained as still as the ship carcasses behind them.

"Their mother—?" the American said.

He shrugged, his mouth a lumpy, hardened bulge. "Cancer. Dead." He turned away from her, into the poisonous, erosive wind. "I was going to leave you, the three of you, out here—*strand* you—for the night. Then return the next morning to ask how you felt about your proposals for us now."

The American said nothing.

"I knew by doing that to you—I knew I would be punished, Professor Reese. This word *punished* means—this means something else to us, I'm afraid, than it does to you. But I felt it was important. Doing something more than—" He stopped himself and turned back to her, smiling again, and pointed at the dune buggy. The driver sat behind the wheel, his back to the wind, smoking. "That is my brother, Ilhomjon. He will care for my children. I leave them to him now."

The American said nothing.

The man hooked his arms around the children and slowly led them away. He stopped, turned to the American, and hesitated before asking her, "It wouldn't have mattered, would it? If I had showed the Americans."

"No," she said.

Now the man nodded. For a long time he nodded. Then he said, "I think I will strand you anyway, Professor," and walked away.

Expensive
Trips Nowhere

Jayne breaks the morning's long silence: "I have a rock in my boot, I think."

Viktor and Douglas do not look at each other as Jayne hunkers into a lotus and with one pull dissolves an impressive knot of signal-orange laces. She removes her boot, turns it upside down, and gives it an irate ketchup-bottle shake. An incisor-shaped pebble plinks off her thigh.

When they continue on, it seems to Douglas that the silence has an entirely new implication. It reminds him of the equally unanswerable silence he and Jayne once shared, walking side by side to Lenox Hill Hospital after he'd accidentally broken her arm playing touch football with friends in Central Park. To speak, then as now, struck him as absurd.

A moraine-pocked valley sprawls before him beneath the cloudy dimmer of a huge gray sky. A powerless yellow blur is the only indication that the sun continues to exist. Jayne is ahead of him now, moving up the valley's gentle slope, hopping from boulder to boulder, her little brown ponytail bouncing. Viktor is in the lead. Far in the lead. Too far, Douglas thinks, popping an herbal cough drop. The valley and surrounding mountains are so quiet that the accumulated jingle of their equipment has the star-tling tonality of a triangle tapped over and over again.

When Douglas closes his eyes, his skull filling with peppermint, he thinks of the *tink* of silverware at wordless meals spent with his parents and of childhood carriage rides through a powdery Central Park. But his lids lift and he is back on the steppe, moving across the world's empty center.

By leaping from rock to rock to rock in their quest to reach the valley's other side, Douglas understands that he and Jayne and Viktor are engaged in what is known as *bouldering,* a term that strikes Douglas as one rich with effortful coinage. He has bouldered before; this is their second boulder field of the day. They came upon their first early this morning, long before their run-in with the bandits, passing through a talus-littered cleft to find themselves at the base of a forbidding muskeg pitted with rocky islets, the unrisen sun a pink smear along the horizon. Some boulders were Volkswagen-sized, others no bigger than an ottoman. They lay fixed in the valley's spring-thawed soil and stretched for nearly a mile, forming by some glacial fluke a workable path. Viktor had been quick to provide navigational pointers.

Keep your feet in center of any rock you step on. Otherwise you roll rock and turn your ankle. Step only on rocks with fur.

Douglas and Jayne had exchanged glances. *Lichens, you mean?*

Da, da. Lichens. Old rocks, he'd said. *Most secure.*

When Viktor finished, his indifferent powder-blue eyes locked on Douglas's. *Ponimayete?* he asked him.

Understand? Douglas had nodded, irritated by Viktor's insistence on addressing him in Russian before the clarifying English switch-over. There is something malevolent about this, Douglas decides now.

Douglas watches Jayne maneuver along the rocks, wondering in a distracted way exactly what anatomical principle causes her rear end to double in size when she bends over. Jayne, it seems, has taken Viktor's instruction to heart; any time her feet wander out to a boulder's periphery, they spark immediately back to the center. Standing there, features scrunched, fussing with her backpack straps, her ponytail stilled, she spends the same amount of time settling on her next boulder as she does selecting fruit at the market. When she moves, though, she moves with beautiful simian grace, and only now can Douglas picture Jayne as the freckly, tree-climbing tomboy she claims to have once been. Some inner perversity moves Douglas to venture only to those boulders Jayne has dismissed. Once aboard a particularly chancy reject—a wobbly-looking anvil-shaped rock naked of any lichens whatsoever—Douglas, emboldened by transgression, pushes his waffled black boot sole right to the boulder's edge.

When Douglas cries out, Viktor calmly takes a seat and smokes an Okhotnichny cigarette. Jayne, perhaps twenty meters away, squats on a large rock with one hand pressed across her mouth. Through a mesh of fingers she asks her husband if he is all right.

The man pulls off his backpack and muddy, thickly sopping boot and sits down, rubbing his woolen foot.

"Ankle," he tells her, grimacing. Then, quickly, he calls to Viktor, "I'm all right," and waves, once, as though forcefully wiping something from a blackboard. The idiot has turned his ankle. Of course. Viktor had decided long before the bandits that he does not much like this Douglas. He rarely respects his clients, though he often comes to tolerate them. For two hundred dollars a day, Viktor has found, most people can be tolerated quite easily. But not this Douglas. A large, soft, American oaf.

"Doug, honey," the woman says, shooting Viktor a quick look before turning back to her husband. It is the first conversation they have had, as far as Viktor knows, since the bandits. "Can you walk?"

The man is now holding his ankle with two hands, as though strangling it. He looks up at her, his cheeks lit with a burgundy glow. Sweat plasters his clipped black bangs to his forehead. His eyes are watery blurs, as though he has eaten something tiny, red, and hot. He is in some pain, obviously. "I can walk. Just—just give me a second."

The woman nods and looks back at Viktor. She stands, hugging herself. Her head is small and egg-shaped, her brown eyebrows as dense as hedges. Her face has the taut, squinty intensity Viktor knows well: the look of a worried American woman trying very hard to appear that she has seen it all. Jayne is short and, Viktor thinks, disappointing. Hard stocky legs. Medium-length camel-brown hair. Small muscular arms, like a *kishlak* boy's. Viktor can only imagine what taking such a tiny powerful thing might be like. Disappointing, he thinks. It is all very disappointing.

"Do you think they'll come back?" she asks Viktor.

Viktor stubs out his cigarette and deposits its accordioned husk into the breast pocket of his khaki vest. He shrugs. "Is difficult to say."

"They're not coming back," Douglas says. He is no longer holding his ankle but simply sitting there, his long inert legs hanging off the boulder's edge and his yellow marshmallowy Gore-Tex vest unzipped. Beneath his vest is a shadow-blue T-shirt affixed with a plain black Batman logo. ("The *old* Batman logo, from the forties," Douglas had been careful to point out to Viktor, when Viktor asked about it, which feels to Viktor like a very long time ago.) Douglas's head is tipped back to the sunless sky, his eyes are closed, and his temples pulse as he pulverizes another cough drop.

Jayne looks back at her husband and sighs through her nose. Beneath her pack, her shoulders sag and her spinal column wishbones outward, as though respiration and posture had some complicated association. "Doug—"

"They're *not.*" The second word is as propulsive as a round. Jayne rocks back a little, so stunned she is nearly smiling. Instantly Douglas shakes his head, an apology he seems to recognize is too impersonal to mean anything.

Jayne turns away, trolling her eyes across a motionless sea of rock. She has spent the last four days in such constant close contact with Douglas that intimacy's pleasant burden now feels more like a millstone. The twenty-four-hour flight from JFK to Frankfurt to Almaty. The two days they'd spent sightseeing in Almaty, trying valiantly to pretend that Almaty had two days' worth of sights to see.

95

They'd bused from their hotel to the world's largest ice rink at Medeo and skated beside ex–Soviet hockey stars. They'd traipsed through Panfilov Park and watched dozens of solemn old Kazakhs play chess in the murky sunshine. They'd scratched Zenkov Cathedral—which claimed to be the tallest wooden building in the world—from their pitiful itinerary. They drank fermented mare's milk in a fast-food restaurant shaped like a yurt, ate blocky tomato sandwiches and apples as big as softballs at the Zelyony Bazaar, and wandered back to their room, killing time with the BBC as they waited for the Hotel Kazakhstan's sixty minutes of hot-water service, which commenced at the supremely inconvenient hour of 5 p.m.

They are here for no real reason. Two years ago, Jayne found herself with Douglas ducking her way inside something called Glowworm Cave in Waitomo, New Zealand. Last year she'd had her photograph taken beside Hadrian's Arch in Jarash, Jordan. Both were what Douglas called Expensive Trips Nowhere, the rubric beneath which this current junket also falls. Douglas first conceived of the Expensive Trip Nowhere after his parents were blind-sided on the New Jersey Turnpike by an Atlantic City–bound tour bus whose driver had suffered a stroke at the wheel. Douglas and Jayne had been married a little shy of a year when it happened. Jayne had stabilized into a teeth-clenched toleration of Douglas's parents, Park-and-Seventieth gentry who never understood why their son had settled for "some mousy midwestern girl." This was the phrase Douglas had once quoted—his ill-advised attempt at honesty—in trying to provide Jayne with some understandable frame for his parents' animosity.

Douglas did not seem surprised that his parents had ceded their estate to a number of New York charitable organizations rather than to him. His parents had, however, arranged for a *dispositive provision*—thus began Jayne's education in the phraseology of bequeathment— which ensured that a portion of their trust's income and dividends would be paid out monthly to Douglas, a "sum certain" to the tune of $8,000. Beyond that not a cent belonged to him, except in cases of "extreme need," and only then in "reasonable amounts," along with other similar caveats that kept the world in suspended litigation.

The monthly windfall was large enough to encourage carelessness yet modest enough to make frugality seem picayune. Months after the accident, in bed one night, at some namelessly late hour, neither of them sleeping, both of them knowing it, her back discreetly to him, Douglas proposed the Expensive Trip Nowhere, a journey to no place, for no reason, with no plan. Just to go. Just to leave. He spoke with such irreproachable sadness that Jayne rolled over to find his eyes pooled. She'd agreed, instantly. She knew that Douglas's wealthy Manhattan upbringing had been far too serious a matter to allow for even the suggestion of a childhood; rather like a sexually timid girl turning incandescent atop a boy she finally trusts, the death of his parents now allowed Douglas the consort of some unfamiliar, someday self he'd always been denied.

Three months ago, Douglas had burst into their

apartment blabbing about Kazakhstan, from which one of his uniformly affluent students' parents had just returned. Jayne, whose purse had been stolen in New Zealand and who had been extravagantly ill in Jordan (or, as she called it, *Giardian*), stood there in their kitchen, holding a stack of DoubleStuf Oreos that she had spent a good part of the day stevedoring into her mouth, staring at Douglas with a slipping, ugly expression she hated him for not heeding.

The next day Douglas came home with a muddy fax from something called the Adventure Mountain Company in Almaty, Kazakhstan's largest city. It offered two- or four-day package tours of hiking, rock climbing, rafting, and other communions with the natural world of which Douglas knew nothing. She read over the fax, numb. "Come on," he'd wheedled. And suddenly he was Douglas again, her rescuer from Manhattan starving artistry. "You're a Midwesterner, Jayney. Aren't you supposed to *like* this stuff?"

Douglas was never embarrassed to be an American, never hesitant to reveal his monolingual helplessness. Wherever he found himself, he pumped hands with street vendors and enjoyed an incorruptible digestive system. Travel scraped him away to reveal not some dulled surface but bright new layers of personality. But Jayne is thirty years old. She wishes to learn nothing new about the man she married. That time is gone. It has been months since she has even attempted a sculpture, a career that has earned her a reliable five-figure salary, provided that one counted past the decimal points. This was her joke for the cocktail-party circuit.

Jayne now studies the plain, awful hurt on Douglas's face. It is a large lumpy face above which a periwig would not seem at all improper. The bluish beginnings of a spotty, erratic beard gleam upon his cheeks and chin like an unfinished tattoo. His boot is beside him, encased in a cracked shell of mud. She catches herself thinking, *Ruined.* The boots I bought for him are ruined. And she knows that for one horrible moment she has forgotten that he is hurt, or does not care, which is the same thing. This is marriage, she thinks, with a whelm of heartsick apathy. This is what happens. Its intimacy is such that you—

"God," Jayne says suddenly, paddling her hands in front of her face. Some of Viktor's cigarette smoke has, in the motionless air, drifted to her nostrils and given her lungs a toxic baptism. She looks over at Viktor. "What on *earth* are you smoking?"

Viktor flashes a horselike smile. He has a pure Slavic face that allows Jayne to grasp what *Caucasian* really means. The arches of his cheeks look as hard as whetstones. His hair is stalky and yellow, like wheat. It occurs to her that only Caucasian follicles pigment their yield with something other than humanity's standard-issue black.

"Death in swamp," Viktor answers her. "Very strong. Very bad taste. Is what we call them."

Jayne obliges him. "We?"

"Afghantsi," he says.

Jayne nods blithely and looks back to Douglas, who is staring at Viktor with huge confounded eyes.

"Afghantsi?" Douglas says, his tone one of vague challenge.

Viktor nods sharply, then stands. "*Da*. Come. Replace your boot. We walk again."

"What," Jayne asks Douglas after Viktor has forged out ahead, "is an Afghantsi?"

Douglas reaches out to Jayne and she pulls him onto her boulder, releasing his hand the moment he is balanced. Douglas's ankle feels vulcanized, though he has tied his laces so tightly he cannot quite claim that it hurts. He shrugs at Jayne. "That means he's a veteran."

Jayne stares into some middle distance, her chest heaved out. Stray coils of premature gray wisp around her small shell-like ears. "A veteran of what?"

"The Soviet war in Afghanistan."

They both look at Viktor. He has stopped ten boulders up and waits for them with a lavishly dour face and his arms in a tight cross-chest plait. Jayne stares at him, her lips scarcely moving as she speaks. "And these Afghantsi all smoke the same awful cigarettes?"

"Looks that way."

"Great," she says, leaping to the next rock.

⸻

"Your coat," Viktor asks Jayne. "How much you pay?"

They are walking across a greenish hillock, pingo mounds squishing beneath their boots. The boulder field is an hour's walk behind them. The clouds have broken, and sunlight falls upon the steppe in huge warm rhomboids. The lower slopes of the Tien Shan Mountains are smoky with the vapor of spring-melted snow, and their white saw-toothed upper slopes and horns glitter like pyrite. Jayne walks beside Viktor, while Douglas has dropped back.

Jayne looks down at her orange jacket. It is a Patagonia Puffball jacket, space-agey and shiny, tricked out with Polarguard HV insulation, a ripstop nylon shell, and water-resistant coating. She purchased it and her Patagonia Capalene underwear, her Dana Design Glacier backpack, her Limmer hiking boots, her Helly Hansen rain pants, and her EMS Traverse sleeping bag at Paragon on Eighteenth and Broadway a few weeks after they booked their flight on Kazair. She can't remember what the jacket had set her back specifically, but remembers quite well the $1,200 dent the excursion bashed into her checking account. She feigns recollection. "Fifty dollars?"

Viktor eyes her suspiciously, a Grand Inquisitor of sportswear. "I ask another American about her coat. Same color. Patagonia. She tells that she pay three hundred dollars."

"It was on sale," Jayne says quietly, then stops to wait for Douglas.

Viktor smirks as he fishes the half-smoked cigarette from his breast pocket. As he lights up the remnant, he remembers his schoolboy days as group leader of his Oktyabryata youth group, back when he wore his bright red Young Pioneer scarf nightly to bed, still glowing from the *A* he'd received in Scientific Communism for his critique of bourgeois individualism at School Number 3. This was before he knew of such things as Patagonia jackets. Before, as a private in the Signal Corps stationed near Kandahar, he went out on patrol as a demonstrably Soviet soldier and returned equipped with the battlefield tackle of half the planet's nations. After scavenging the bodies of dead *mujahideen*, his platoon's medics threw away their Soviet-made syringes, rendered magically sterile by a thin paper wrapping, and stocked up on Japanese disposable syringes whose plungers never clogged. Their Soviet plasma containers, half-liter glass bottles that shattered constantly, were exchanged for captured Italian-made polyethylene liter blood bags so rupture-resistant one could stomp on them in field boots to no effect. Their Soviet flak jackets were so heavy many soldiers could barely lift them. Upon seizing their first American flak jacket, Viktor's mystified platoon found that this vestment, which lacked a single metal part, could not be penetrated at point-blank range with a Makarov pistol. He did not know, then, that when the war began the *muj* were armed only with cheap Maxim rifles you could not fire for long without scorching your guide hand. He did not know of the CIA and ISI airlifts and border sanctuaries the *muj* were then making use of. His schoolboy critique of bourgeois individualism did not foresee such contingencies any more than the Americans who would one day pay him to safeguard their leisure. But he feels little pleasure in having shamed the woman over her jacket. He lied to her about knowing its true price. He has several such jackets at home, which he wears only around the cafés of Almaty for the status their indiscreet labels supply.

"Hey," Douglas says, as he falls in beside Jayne.

"Hey," Jayne returns.

Douglas's mouth goes tight, his mustache of sweat sparkling. "Are we there yet?"

She motions toward his foot. "How's that ankle?"

"Okay. It just hurts. That's good, though, right? When it stops hurting is when you're in trouble."

A small, toothless smile. "That's frostbite."

"Well. The good news then is that I don't have frostbite."

Jayne digs into her jacket's marsupial pocket and removes a cling-wrapped piece of crumbly halvah. She holds it out to Douglas, who shakes his head. Jayne takes a bite, several hundred sesame seeds instantly installing themselves between her teeth. She looks across the steppe, a sweep of land so huge and empty she wonders if a place can be haunted by an *absence* of ghosts. She has never seen a sky so big. So big, in fact, it makes her own pathetic smallness somehow gigantic—as though to contemplate one's place in the nothingness of the universe can only set free some stoned homunculus of monomania.

"Walking here," she tells Douglas suddenly, "I can't get something out of my mind. It just repeats itself over and over again. What's weird is that it's a poem."

"That's not weird." His tone hovers just above annoyance.

She looks over at him, noting the new crease in his forehead. "Not if you're an English teacher. Normal people don't walk around with poems in their heads."

"What's the poem?" His tone is curt, satisfied, as though he has just prevailed in some internal argument of which he neglected to make her a part.

She ignores this, finding the loop in her mind and giving it voice: "'Two roads diverged in a yellow wood, / And sorry I could not travel both / And be one traveler, long I stood / And looked down one as far as I could / To where it bent in the undergrowth.'"

"Frost?" he says. "That's even less weird. He's as catchy as a pop song."

"I had to memorize it in fourth grade. If I've thought about it three times since then I'd be surprised."

Douglas stares at his boots and says, almost meditatively, "'Love and forgetting might have carried them / A little further up the mountainside / With night so near, but not much further up.'"

They walk silently for a while, strides synchronized. Jayne finishes her halvah and kisses the honey from her fingertips. "That's . . . really lovely," she says at last.

"Frost again," Douglas says.

She walks out ahead of him, shaking her head in affected wonder. "I've hiked in a lot of places, but never anywhere so big."

"Kazakhstan is five times the size of France."

"That's what I mean. And it's so *empty.*"

Douglas nods. "During Stalin, Kazakhstan was repopulated with Ukrainians and Russians, so much so that they soon outnumbered the Kazakhs. Rather than see their livestock collectivized, the Kazakhs slaughtered something like twenty million sheep and goats, five million cattle, and three million horses."

"Someone's been reading his guidebook."

"Kazakhstan also happened to be the Soviet Union's

atomic playground. From the fifties to the early nineties, fifteen atom bombs a year were exploded over and under Semipalatinsk, which is"—he stops, gets his dubious bearings, and points—"I think about six hundred miles that way. So. You do the math, and it turns out that this place endured over eight hundred nuclear blasts in all. Enough to destroy the entire planet several times over. We haven't avoided a nuclear holocaust as much as localized it in one very unlucky place."

"Which explains perfectly why you're lecturing *me.*"

The bleakness of her tone stops him dead. "I'm—" He can't get a word out; his throat is lined with thorns. He breathes until the pent sentence finally bursts free. "I'm *not* lecturing you. I can't *believe* you think I'm lecturing you." But now, of course, he is.

Jayne is walking fast now, as upright as a sea horse. "I'd like to thank you again for bringing me here," Douglas hears her say.

And then he is walking by himself, just as Jayne is, just as Viktor is. Three strangers on the steppe. Douglas feels the special bitter pleasure that comes with being angry and righteous and alone. She could leave him. He knows that. It is one of the many things he knows. He knows that he is a teacher because he enjoys the attention of children more than that of adults, and he knows there is something egotistical and sinister and frightened in this enjoyment. He knows that once, when he was haunting Lower Manhattan bookstores in the wake of his law-school washout, Jayne had found him irresistible and strange but now finds him something else but has not yet fully figured out what, he doesn't think. He knows poetry, all about poetry—Frost, Auden, Stevens—and had—briefly!—tried to write it, but he knows he is no good, and this does not bother him, much. He knows nothing about IPOs and 401(k)s. He also knows he is in possession of no special gift, no appreciable talent, a peasant in the New Economy's fiefdom, and that his parents, whose living disapproval had once made this condition acceptable, are dead. And he knows, too, that he is a coward.

Viktor and Jayne have stopped at a small hill twenty yards ahead. They are turned toward him and stand in rugged colored silhouette against scalloped mountains and an icy blue sky. Douglas looks up, toward the sun. The morning's earlier cumulus ceiling has now fully dissipated, and thin lenticular saucer clouds float across the atmosphere. He trudges up the hill and, once he has joined them, hears a gush as thick as applause coming from its opposite side.

"A river," Jayne says. For some reason, she smiles. He looks to Viktor and wonders what they were talking about but does not really wish to know.

"Oh," Douglas says. "Okay." He casts his eyes to the base of the hill and sees the river, a rush of silver topped with turbulent foam.

"Doesn't look so bad," Jayne offers mildly.

"Rivers," Viktor intones. "Very dangerous. We cross!" He charges down the hill. Jayne watches Viktor with pallid awe. His movements have a thoughtless, animal anticipation, seemingly privy to the terrain's every secret. Viktor transfers his weight from one foot to the other so smoothly that gravity seems to pull him forward rather than down. Although it is spring and the steppe is still cold, Viktor wears dirty canvas shorts. This allows Jayne to note his grenadelike calves and the long pythonic muscles on the backs of his thighs. Jayne remembers, abruptly, that Russian men are famed ballet dancers.

"Once more into the breach," Douglas mutters, galloping down the hill himself. Jayne feels something uncomfortably close to disappointment that Douglas makes it to the bottom without stumbling. She ventures down the hill herself, slowly and sideways, like a crab.

After a moment of double-check reconnoitering, Viktor leads them along the river's bank. It is edged with rocks and mucky soil and vaguely pubic gray-green vegetation and not a speck of evidence that human beings had ever before walked this path. Long white phalanges of snow lie in every shady furrow. "We must find widest part," Viktor tells them.

Douglas shouts over the rage of the river, "Why don't we just cross right now?"

Viktor turns to answer, but Jayne beats him to it. "Wherever the river is widest is also where the current is slowest." She finds a stick marooned between two rocks at river's edge and, to illustrate her point, heaves it into the water. The stick is caught and swept away more quickly than even she was expecting.

Douglas shakes his head, either angry he is wrong or angry she has made him so. He calls to Viktor, "You knew the river was here, though, right? Why didn't you lead us . . . *around* it?"

"Once, river small," he responds, without turning around. "Now river big."

Douglas laughs, a cosmically empty laugh. "What does *that* mean?"

Viktor stops, head darkly tipped forward, then turns to confront him. His face has a clear unwrinkled menace. His mouth is open but he says nothing, his tongue dry and gray in its hollow. It is as though whole paragraphs of choice, partially translated reproaches are cycling through his Russian brain.

Suddenly Jayne is wedging herself between them. "The snow, you mean? The snow melted and ran down from the mountains?"

Viktor blinks. His mouth closes and stretches into a grin that doesn't seem to end. He claps, once, joylessly, and sets off again, all marching-past-the-Kremlin energy.

"You two are certainly hitting it off," Douglas tells her, when Viktor is out of earshot. The words do not hang between them for long before he feels a cold tremor of regret. Amazing, he thinks: He really could not have said anything worse. He tries to launder the statement with a joke, softly elbowing her and hating the falseness of the smile tearing his lips away from his teeth. "Should I worry about going back home alone?"

Jayne takes a long time to respond, a silence in which Douglas hears her die to him three, four, five times. "I wonder if you *would* worry about that."

Douglas puts up a monitory hand. "Okay. Let's stop now." He walks for a while, kicking every bit of rock not bolted down by erosion into the river. "It would worry me. It would kill me. You know that."

Jayne says nothing. Douglas listens to her breathe, inhales the thin unpleasant scent coming off her unwashed body. She did not use to smell like this, not even after spending a whole day in bed with him. He wonders at what age it is exactly that women exchange their scent of talc for that of faint decay. Just as he begins to hold this against her, Douglas winces, his ankle knocking like a pinched blood vessel. The only thing that keeps him from stopping to tighten his bootlaces is the certainty that Jayne will not wait for him if he does.

Viktor drops his pack and turns to them. "We cross," he announces gravely.

"This doesn't look any wider," Douglas mutters to no one, bending down to redo his laces. When he is finished he looks at the river and sees that, actually, it *is* a bit wider here. On top of that, a dozen well-placed rocks make a broken span from one side of the river to the other. There is probably not a better place to cross a river in the entire former Soviet Union.

Viktor stands next to his huge torso-sized pack, contemplating the river. Jayne unloads her much smaller pack and sets it beside Viktor's. Viktor's pack is as gray and beaten as Almaty concrete; it appears better suited to haul potatoes than carry gear. Jayne's pack, Douglas notes, is offensively new and colored in laboratory hues of yellow and red and orange. When Jayne squats beside Viktor, her thighs spreading like thick flanks of beef, Douglas turns away.

He walks over to the river's edge and ponders the radioactivity that in all likelihood lurks along this riverbed's freezing silt. He imagines all of Kazakhstan's rivers as great glowing veins carrying their ghastly chemotherapy to the nation's every corner. That there is something catastrophically wrong right before his eyes, something he can do nothing to alleviate or worsen, fills him with almost holy relief.

Jayne stares at her pack, condemned by its newness. She feels Viktor's cold Russian eyes on her. "Please don't look at me," Jayne says softly, pulling the elastic cinch from the back of her head. Her ponytail comes apart, pungent oily hair falling into her downturned face. She blinks away the strands that catch in the barbed wire of her eyelashes.

Viktor nudges her pack with his boot, knocking his hands together in cryptic anticipation. She turns. His hands are eye-level, huge and chalky and cracked, his knuckles like rivets. "Steppe makes strong what is strong," Viktor says. "Makes weak what is weak."

She shakes her head. "Viktor, please. Spare me." When she looks back at him he is gone, leaping across the river.

Douglas wanders over to Jayne, still squatting by her pack. "More boulders, huh?" Jayne's eyebrows raise with crushing politeness. Douglas looks at Viktor and squints. "What's he doing?"

"Making sure it's safe?"

Douglas snorts and stares at a newfound rock. "Well, bully for him."

"You're having fun." Jayne is still looking away, toward the river's unimaginable headwaters. Fifty yards upstream is a miniature waterfall, the river pouring itself from one level to another in a clean glass-white arc that appears solid enough to walk upon.

He looks down at her. "I don't know what I'm supposed to say about this morning."

Her expression does not change. "You don't have to say anything, Doug."

Quickly he squats beside her. "You know that if they did *anything* to you—"

She nods in hard, quick countermeasure, her eyes awash with unhappiness. "I know. I don't want to talk about it."

Douglas looks over to see Viktor returning. His above-the-knee shorts are fringed with a dark watermark and his leather hiking boots have the soaked, deep-brown look of living cowflesh. His legs glisten hairlessly. "*Tak,*" he says, approaching them. "Very important. You keep pack loose when you cross, *da?*"

"Loose?" Jayne says.

Viktor lifts his pack with one hand, as though it were no heavier than a stole. He threads his arms through its straps and buckles his waist belt and sternum strap. Then, in moron-befitting slow motion, he unbuckles his waist belt and sternum strap and lets them dangle meaningfully from his body. "Understand? No straps. Very dangerous."

"No straps," Douglas says, struggling beneath his pack to rise.

"You fall in, you leave pack."

"Right," Douglas says. "I get it."

"No straps."

Douglas's face fills with heat, as though he is leaning into a cleansing steam of dishwasher waft. "Drowning being what we're avoiding here."

Viktor regards Douglas with a vinegary expression, then shakes his head and stalks off toward the river.

"I'm not an idiot, you know," Douglas calls after him.

Viktor slows but does not turn and then continues on.

Jayne is standing now, angrily working her way into her pack. Each word from her mouth seems to sizzle. "Is it a good idea to make an enemy of the one guy who can lead us out of here?"

Douglas looks at her, serenely undoing his straps. "The helicopter picks us up tomorrow. In fifteen hours we'll never see him again."

Viktor gazelles across the river in eight confident bounds. Viktor has that, Douglas thinks: perfect confidence. All thoroughly second-rate people had it. Only once, on the very first rock, was Viktor forced to break stride. Douglas had noted that hesitation and stands on that rock now. Four—possibly five—feet lie between it and the next rock. Douglas grinds his boot waffle against stone, aware that Jayne is waiting behind him, on the bank, as impassive as one of the sculptures in her studio. He is not afraid—the river does not look all that deep; the current *does* seem to let up here—but he knows he cannot fail. He cannot. To do so will allow Viktor to believe any number of things about Douglas, many of which Douglas would ordinarily concede as true. But he is more than the steppe. He is more than this morning. Moments mean nothing. Spume collects on Douglas's face. Viktor now waits on the other side of the river. He sits Indian-style, gallingly oblivious, forearms draped across his knees, a cigarette dangling from his lip like an icicle. Bastard, Douglas thinks. Insolent bastard.

"Doug?" Jayne says.

He half turns. "I didn't say anything while I was waiting for you on those fucking boulders."

Douglas jumps before she can say anything else. His feet come down on rock, blessedly solid. The next few are as simple as walking, and he takes them with Christlike calm. He hops off the last rock, relishing the crunch of his boots in the pebbly ford, and saunters right up to where Viktor is sitting. In oppressive silence Douglas towers above Viktor, cloaking him with his shadow.

Viktor's eyes flick irritably from Douglas to the river to Douglas and then Viktor is standing. He throws his cigarette aside like a dart. Douglas's fists transform into mallets and he struggles free from his pack. But Viktor rushes past him, toward the river. Douglas turns. Splashing. Water in the air. Suddenly Viktor is standing next to Jayne, his hands cupping her small shoulders with unseemly intimacy. Jayne is sopping wet, every limb, every fiber, every part of her. Her waterlogged jacket looks so heavy it seems capable of foundering both of them. Her hair falls around her face in thick buds. She is crying, explaining something, pointing back toward the bank and then at the rock and now she is slapping at the water, which is deep, up to her waist at least, and it is fast. Viktor has braced himself against the river's force, the water churning whitely at his thighs. Viktor lifts Jayne's backpack from the river, water pouring from its innumerable pockets. Jayne's teeth chatter as harshly as dice in a wooden box. She is still speaking when Viktor scoops her up and carries her toward the shore, her wet, frightened face pressed against his chest. Douglas stands at the bank, arms out, waiting for a delivery that never arrives, uselessly conscious of the play of a thousand rainbows on the water and in the air.

In monastic silence they set up camp on a hill a few kilometers from the river, unrolling the downy logs of their sleeping bags and pounding their tent pegs into the taiga. Jayne hangs her wool socks and pants and orange jacket around their glowing portable Daewoo stove, which, here on the treeless steppe, must serve as a campfire. She ducks into their tent and emerges wearing her black rain pants, Douglas's Green Lantern T-shirt, and a yellow windbreaker. She sits down across from Douglas, expressionless. Viktor putters around the camp's edges, as patient as a vulture, then unearths their dinner from his gear. They eat sardines and crackers and sip cognac. After a while they find themselves, still hungry, beneath a bright, freakishly starry sky. For close to an hour Douglas stares at them stare into the stove, then stands. His tent's zipper howls like a moonstruck animal.

Some time later, Douglas hears low, furtive voices. In the vast darkness, the Daewoo throws off a surprising amount of light, and the tent's walls are a molten orange. On one wall Viktor and Jayne's huge golem shadows glower. Douglas is in his sleeping bag, a shiny silver sleeve pleated with cushiony squares. The sleeping bag is said to offer protection up to −40 degrees Fahrenheit. Barring intergalactic travel, he cannot imagine why such protection is necessary. Tomorrow is their last morning on the steppe, he thinks. Tomorrow they will awaken for the last time in the sub-Saharan humidity of this tent's womb. Tomorrow they will rendezvous with the helicopter and for $300 an hour they will be ferried back to Almaty, board a plane, and fly home. Douglas thinks about tomorrow, his awareness crumbling, his eyes gliding shut. Outside, he hears Viktor and Jayne's voices rise a little, his mind suspended in the sandy place between sleep and lucidity.

"What animal are you talking about?" Jayne asks.

"It is bird," Viktor says. "Very . . . beautiful bird. I have seen pictures, photographs of such bird. So beautiful. Is American bird. Its feathers green, and . . . *kak, oranzhivye?*"

"Orange?"

"*Da.* O-range. Red. Yellow. Very beautiful. I want very badly to see this bird fly. I think about this bird much. In Russian we call this bird *utka.* I wonder what word in English must this bird be called. And then I learn that in America you call this bird *duck.* You laugh at me now."

"No, no. I'm just—I've never thought of it that way, I guess. Your English is . . . very good, Viktor."

"*Nyet.* My English is . . . *uzhasny.* Very bad. Idiot English."

Douglas is closer to sleep now, brain waves prenatally flattened. He finds himself cast backward, to this morning, minutes after clearing their first boulder field. He is looking up at a gunmetal overcast sky, wondering if it will rain. Jayne is beside him, talking, though he is listening only enough to offer appropriate grunted interjections. Suddenly he feels Jayne's fingers stab into his wrist, above his watch. His eyes drop.

Viktor is standing fifteen feet ahead of them, frozen. Three men are approaching. Two are not men at all but teenagers. The man is wearing a knockoff Adidas tracksuit and carrying a small antiquated pistol, three of his fingers wrapped around the stock and the fourth extended, casually perpendicular to the breech. One of the boys carries a large curved knife. His face is dirty in the permanent way that suggests poverty, not circumstance. On his long-sleeved sweatshirt is a version of the Chicago Bulls logo so completely mistaken Douglas feels almost sorry for the boy. In Almaty's bazaars he had seen similarly ludicrous permutations: New York Yankees T-shirts which somehow incorporated into their design the Empire State Building, Dallas Cowboy knit hats emblazoned with a single red star, sweatshirts for nonexistent clubs like the Las Vegas Braves and Illinois Champions. All stitched from careless memory and a deep, nameless want—the least cynical piracy he has ever seen.

The man with the pistol lifts his empty hand, and the boys come to a militaristic halt several feet behind him. From the trio's black hair and papyrus-colored skin and almond eyes Douglas knows they are Kazakh. They are smiling.

"What was it like," Jayne asks Viktor outside Douglas's tent, "when you got back?"

"I had to sell my sunglasses! This in Tashkent. *Demobilizatsiya* were sent there, after. No instructions. You understand. Our photos were destroyed. Our letters destroyed. We could not talk about Afghanistan. Illegal, *tak*?"

"Yes. Illegal."

"I had to sell my sunglasses for ticket to Alma-Ata. Now Almaty, then Alma-Ata. I was private, only. Signal Corps. Brute with iron fist! That is what our sergeant say to us. If we do not yell back same loud enough, we are given hole training."

"Hole training."

"*Da.* This is very interesting. You yell into dirty toilet with sergeant behind you. If you don't yell back same loud enough, he push in your face. I ask my mother in Alma-Ata soon to buy me small dog and name it Sergeant so I can strangle small dog when I get home. You laugh at me another time."

"I'm sorry. That's a little funny, though."

"So I wait at train station in Tashkent, and I watch pretty girls in blouses and short skirts. I drink vodka so cold it is like cream. I think of Pavel, my friend, when he wakes up to see his leg cut off by doctors. His face like little girl's, all pink and white. I think of donkeys in Kandahar, how they sit down during shelling, then rise and walk away when shelling stop. That is what I think of Afghanistan then and now. Here. More cognac. Drink."

Viktor greets the Kazakhs in a friendly voice. Douglas looks over at Jayne. Her face is impassive, though her fingers have taloned even deeper into Douglas's wrist. Douglas does not believe Viktor is speaking Russian to them—these harsh, gargly syllables sound nothing like Russian—and this seems to Douglas a cunning tactic indeed. Yes. That's good, isn't it? Engage them on their home court. He notices that Viktor keeps stepping between them and the man with the pistol. He does this casually, artfully, and the man seems simultaneously disinterested and utterly intent on getting a look at them.

One of the teenagers steps away from his comrades, to his left, a large comical cartoonlike step, and peeks around Viktor's shoulder at Douglas. Half a decade logged in classrooms triggers the Pavlovian workings of Douglas's face: he smiles. The boy instantly breaks into Viktor and the man's conversation, chattering and pointing at Douglas. Douglas's chin lifts, his chest expands. He will not give them the comfort of terror, even as his stomach distends with what feels like ice cream and razor blades. But no. The boy is not pointing at Douglas, he realizes. He is pointing at Jayne.

"When bullet hits man," Viktor tells Jayne, "you hear it. Very strange sound. Like slap. You fall down in sand and you look over at your friend and you see the cigarette you gave him three minute ago is still in his teeth."

"I can't imagine that. I can't imagine *any* of this."

"What I remember most is little boy, little *muj,* running at our APC with Molotov cocktail. With our guns we turn him into nothing. Nothing."

"That's—how did that make you feel?"

"I never had problem. Dying is hard. Killing much easier, even for three rubles a month. Tell me why as twenty-year-old I can kill and now I cannot? Children have no pity. That is reason why. Think of their fairy tales. Many death in fairy tales. Baba Yaga cooks little girls in her oven, and children never frightened. They don't cry."

"Fairy tales used to scare me to death. I cried. I cried all the time."

"After little *muj*, my friend buys urine from medics. Urine with . . . hepatitis, *tak*? He drinks urine, he get sick, he go home. Back to Georgia. Very smart friend. War make good men better, and I think make bad men much worse."

Zhoq, Viktor tells them, as the boy points at Jayne and the man with the pistol nods and nods. *Zhoq, zhoq.* Douglas suspects that in Kazakh this means *No* and hopes deeply that he is correct. For the first time, Viktor sounds angry. The man sneers and taps his pistol against his tracksuited leg. Viktor steps close to the man and says something, something hard and final, then looks at the ground. This is a ploy, and Douglas knows it: Viktor's mind throws off a sudden telepathic thunder. They are silent, all of them, for half a minute. Viktor then sighs and digs into his vest pocket for his cigarettes. He offers the man one. The man takes it. Oddly, the man does not light up but gives the cigarette to one of the boys, who pockets it.

Douglas has no conception of what is being said, for what reason, to what end. A black geyser of frustration pushes its way out of him. Before he can stop himself, Douglas calls out to Viktor: *What do they want?* Jayne's other hand whips around, and now both are clamped around Douglas's wrist.

Viktor turns to Douglas, his face the astonished white of a lanced blister. *Shut up*, he says softly. It sounds to Douglas like *shtup*. At this, the man with the pistol points at himself, furiously, then thrusts his arms out at Douglas. Douglas finds himself studying the flailing pistol. It is fixed on him, now the sky, now the ground, him again. Then the rant is finished. The pistol drops. The man spits at Viktor's feet. The boys laugh. Douglas finds himself thinking of music, of poetry, of themes and motifs building to sensible effect. But life is not like that. Life is chaos. People are horrifyingly alive and unknowable. As if personally escorting this realization from the stable of Douglas's mind, the man walks over to Douglas, shrugging off Viktor's feeble attempt to get in his way. Douglas's knees fill with gelatin. As the man advances, he raises his pistol with almost threatless firing-range composure and points it at Douglas again. The man stops, his wet lips pushed out in curiosity. The pistol's tiny black aperture is twenty inches from Douglas's forehead, and without thought or intention Douglas takes hold of Jayne's shoulders and pushes her in front of him.

Jayne gasps, her face buried in her jacket's shoulder. Douglas lets go of her instantly and steps forward, halving the distance between his forehead and the pistol. His eyes squeeze shut. He does not know where Jayne is. The boys are laughing again. When Douglas opens his eyes he sees that Viktor has materialized next to the man, and he whispers indulgently into his ear. The boy with the knife polishes its curved blade along his thigh.

"Is never the same, after. Never. Many Afghantsi go on killing. Gangsters. Criminals. Hooligans who beat up rock-and-rollers at concerts. I throw my medals into Balkhash after war."

"Do you ever talk to anyone about it?"

"Sometimes I see Afghantsi in Gorky Park. No legs, no arms, and I know them. I say nothing. Soviet Army Day, twenty-three February, they carry flowers and wear their medals and walk through Alma-Ata. That day, only that day, I go to cemetery. We are not buried in military cemetery because we did not fight in war. We fulfilled our international duty. That is what every red tombstone say: DIED IN EXECUTION OF HIS INTERNATIONAL DUTY. But beneath that are other messages, from Mama and Papa and sweethearts. 'Sun and moon extinguished without you, dearest son.' That is on tombstone of my friend Alek Ladutko. Nineteen years old. And on tombstone of Boris Zilfigarov, my friend shot with my cigarette, his sweetheart writes, 'The earth is a desert without you.' I drink to him now."

Viktor has calmed the man. He lowers his pistol, then scratches his temple with its long needlelike barrel. He rubs his chin. He enjoys a series of frowns. At what seems to Douglas precisely the right moment, Viktor's arm finds its way around the man's shoulder and, gently, he guides him away from Douglas and Jayne. When their backs are to them, Douglas does not look at Jayne, nor she at him.

The Kazakhs leave. Agreeably. Suddenly. Saluting Viktor, Viktor saluting back. The three of them trudge off in the direction from which they appeared, and Viktor turns to Jayne and Douglas, one eye squinted shut in the sun.

"Why are you looking at me like that?" Jayne asks Viktor now. "Stop looking at me like that."

"You are very beautiful," Viktor tells her. "I do not have beautiful things in my life."

"I'm not beautiful. I'm awful."

"You say that because your husband is in his tent, listening to us. If he not there, you would not be awful. You would only be beautiful."

"You're awful. You're being awful to me right now. I don't even know if anything you've told me is true."

"The earth is a desert without you. . . ."

"Stop it."

"You sleep with me in my tent tonight. Your oaf is asleep. He will not know. He fails you. Over and over today he fails you. He does not deserve—"

"Have you ever thought, Viktor, that whatever a man says to you, no matter what it is, at some level whatever he's saying to you is just so fucking . . . *poisonous*?"

"I don't understand."

"Of course you don't. I've had too much to drink. Oh, I don't want to sleep. I've had too—"

"I go to tent now. You can join me. Your choose. I could make you. I could kill your oaf now, in his bed. I think maybe he would not mind so much. But I won't do this. Where you sleep is your choose."

Who were they? Jayne had asked.

Bandits, Viktor said, shrugging. On the steppe, such things happen. What could one do? *Bad men.*

What did they want? Douglas had asked, again.

Viktor had looked at him, not unkindly. *I think you no want to know.*

Douglas's eyes flicker open, his mind half conscious of the sudden, growing silence outside his tent. No, he thinks. No, I don't want to know. Not this, not that. Nothing. Nothing and not anything not ever again.

The
Ambassador's
Son

I liked the Capital because you could always find something to do there. Booze, women, dancing—you name it. As for the rest of the country, the guidebook writers could have the place. They didn't even have *toilets* outside the Capital. Please realize I require very little as a human being: bread, water, flush toilet. Something about living on the cusp of the millennium and still shitting over a hole calls into question the entire concept of historical progress.

I'll tell you a little about the country. It was one of the old Soviet republics where you started drinking at ten, started *really* drinking at fifteen, and dropped dead of it around fifty. The kind of place that was so corrupt that you had to bribe yourself to get out of bed in the morning. This wasn't one of the European former Soviet republics; this was one of the Central Asian republics you've never heard of. As for the culture, I'll say this: its combo of Soviet paranoia and Muslim xenophobia made red wine and fish look like peanut butter and jelly in comparison.

You didn't see a whole lot of tourists hanging out in the Capital, needless to say, but there were a few Americans around. (There are always a few Americans around.) First, you had the Professional Expatriates at the embassy. Their ranks were filled with a lot of uptight stuffed shirts, stuffed blouses, stuffed heads. Most of them couldn't stray a block from embassy row without their cell phones, chauffeured cars, and *International Herald Tribune*s. Second, you had your Do-Gooders. These people, God bless them, needed a serious fucking clue. Each fall I'd see a new group of hatchlings turn up in the Capital, their first day in-country, snappily dressed, taking pictures with disposable cameras for Mom and Dad back home in Iowa and Nebraska and Michigan. Then they'd get shipped out to the villages. Three months later I'd see them back in the Capital shopping for Snickers bars and deodorant, crazed and dandruff-ridden. Finally, you had your Sharks, men and women whose in-country presence consisted solely of pocketing ducats. This wasn't as evil as you might think, not even by folksinger standards. After all, the more money the Sharks made, the more the country made, and everyone was happy. Sometimes Sharks were Do-Gooders who'd stayed but gotten wise on how to live; sometimes they were Professional Expats who'd had their fill of embassy politics; and sometimes they were twenty-four-year-old ephebes with liberal arts degrees pulling down seventy-five grand a year as "consultants" for PriceWaterhouse or Boeing or British-American Tobacco. As for me, I had an in-country sinecure but didn't consider myself one of the Sharks. Although I was around the embassy a lot no one would have mistaken me for a Professional Expat. A Do-Gooder, then? Hardly.

I was the ambassador's son.

A dilemma: What do you do when you're sunk to the hilt in the lovely, splayed vagina of bent-over Olga, who to your utter, surprised delight is finger-diddling the lipsticky and raven-haired Svetlana, when suddenly you hear your mother coming down the stairs? Did I mention that these stairs and the darkened basement they lead to are found in a home belonging to the United States embassy? Did I mention you live in this palace, which supplies a chauffeur named Sergei and an idiotically generous stipend? Finally, and most significantly, did I mention you're two caterpillar lengths' away from an orgasm of Vesuvian proportions?

When the lights came on two things struck me. The first was that Olga had an American flag tattooed on her porky left rump cheek. The other was the difficulty of the choice I suddenly faced. The light switch was found halfway down the staircase, so I knew I had a second or two to pull on my pants and do at least a modicum of damage control. But Svetlana was spread-eagled on a large purple leather couch, bent-over Olga was before her on her knees, and I was screwing Olga from behind; this is not an easy situation from which to extricate oneself. In all honesty, I was too close to destroying Pompeii even to have considered stopping. I suppose it would be fairly easy to second-guess my judgment, but I'd never screwed two girls at once. My only defense is that you do not ask Columbus to turn around when the guy in the basket starts screaming "Land ho!"

How long my mother watched before I heard her outraged gasp I'm unsure. I should point out that I love my mother. She'd stuck with my dad through his long, often dreary embassy-to-embassy career. ("A diplomat lives the

life of a dog," Jefferson said, and he was in fucking *Paris*.)
First, until it blew up, he was in Beirut, where Dad was a
staffer; then he spent a tense decade in the Soviet Union,
where Dad was an ambassador's aide; then to Dad's
biggest gig as a press envoy in the U.S. embassy in
Afghanistan, which was about as much fun as you'd think;
and then to his reward, the Capital. My mother was a
woman who made an effort to learn the language of every
country she traveled to. She shopped in the bazaars
shoulder to shoulder with the locals. She *cared*. And this
is what she had to see: an orgasmic Sveta hooting *"Da,
da!"* and slapping the couch cushions with her hands,
Olga's finger rubbing her blood-swollen clit with the
blurry speed of a hummingbird, and me, her son, ejacu-
lating with enough torque to cross my eyes. When I was
done—this process took a bit longer than I would have
liked—I had no choice but to turn to her.

Mom was no shrinking violet. She'd been in bullet-
peppered cars in Beirut and had a rotten cabbage pitched
in her face in Kabul, and by the time we locked pupils
she'd composed herself. She wore a fuzzy white bathrobe
with the American embassy insignia embossed smartly
into the breast. Her hair was flattened and color-drained
to the shade of gray found only in black-and-white movies.
Her eyes were dry and unforgiving. "Oh," she said, except
it was more of a sigh. "Oh, *Alec*."

By now, Olga and Sveta knew the score. They were
huddled naked against each other, whispering in Russian.
I draped a nearby blanket along the three of us, and we sat
there, the girls looking at the floor and me looking at the

girls while my mother shook her head. I didn't care about Olga and Sveta, really. They were Russian strumpets I'd picked up in a nightclub. They didn't care about me, either. All they wanted was a chance at the Alec Schiavo Visa Application Program.

"Mom," I said, vaguely remembering my mother's oath—after my urine had shown simultaneous traces of cocaine, marijuana, and opium—that it would be the Last Time she'd forgive me. She'd made that quite clear—it would be the Last Time, as opposed to the last time. You still have seven or eight "last times" left once you get that first one, but once you're given a Last Time, it's serious. (The drug test was at the request of the embassy's regional security officer, a doughy guy called—not to his face—Genghis Ron, who did not care for me or, as he once put it, my "whole program," one bit.)

"Alec," she said again, closing her eyes, her face hardening.

I figured I had one chance to fix all this, to say the right thing. (Before I tell you what fell out of my mouth I feel it's germane to point out that I'd spent the better part of the evening smoking Afghan poppy seeds that Sveta had seemed really surprised to find in her purse.) I put my arms around the girls, hugged them to me, and said, "Two chicks at *once,* Mom."

In a flash of fuzzy, hazy white, my mother vanished from the staircase. The next thing I knew my ear was twisting between her sharp fingers. She pulled me to my feet, my pants still around my ankles, and dragged me trippingly across the room. At the stairs I turned and saw

Olga and Sveta on the floor, on their backs, kicking into their pirated American blue jeans.

_____

The Hotel Ta-Ta was a nice place. Built by Indian investors—anything built by Soviet architects had a tendency to fall apart—it relieved you of three hundred dollars a night for the privilege of stepping into its marble lobby and sleeping on its crisp, laundered sheets. I could afford it; I could have afforded twice that much.

The next morning, ten steps past the hotel fountain, I saw Sergei, my chauffeur, sitting on the hood of a gleaming, freshly washed white Toyota Land Cruiser, reading the Capital's Russian-language newspaper. The night before he'd helped me haul all my shit into the suite.

"Sergei," I called, waving. *"Zdravstvuite! Kak dela?"*

"Ah, *prekrasno,* Alec," he said, just about extinguishing our shared vocabulary. (I knew roughly enough Russian to fill the backs of two postcards.) Sergei folded his newspaper into a small square and held it pinned under his arm as he opened my door for me.

I fell into the embassy-supplied Land Cruiser's backseat and rubbed my hangover-tenderized temples. Seconds later Sergei was weaving through the traffic on Rashidov Avenue like an out-of-control darning needle.

"Sergei," I said. *"Café, pozhaluista."*

In the rearview mirror his vodka-reddened eyes flicked onto mine. *"Amerikanskoe café, da?"*

"*Da,*" I said, leaning forward. "Sergei. My father. *Moi* . . . um, *otets?*"

"*Da,*" Sergei said, with a solitary nod.

"Where is he? Uh, *gde moi otets?* Do you know?" I knew Ambassador Schiavo had gone to Kiev to a human-rights conference sponsored by all the former Soviet republics. That morning on BBC, though, I'd seen that a bomb threat had ended the conference three days ahead of time. Was he home, did he call, had my mother debriefed him?

"I no know," Sergei said, with the typical shrug that followed all his heroic efforts at English. "My father, I no know where is he." He looked at me again in the mirror. "*Khorosho,* Alec?"

Still, after several months, I was pleased to see the fruits of Sergei's and my daily five-minute English lessons. "*Khorosho,* Sergei. Great. To the café. Me want coffee now chop-chop."

"Chop-chop," Sergei said, shifting, and I sat back and watched the Capital's weird, oppressive architecture fill the spotless square of my window and then, after a moment, slide soundlessly away. I dozed off for a few blocks and woke to the sound of Sergei beeping his horn at a big-bottomed Tatar girl wearing black stretch pants and a tight white T-shirt. She was standing on the corner of the trendiest street in town, the street where one found the New World Café. Sergei turned around, grinning, showing me his mouthful of substitute gold teeth. "Alec," he said, grinning. "Beeg tits, nice ahs, *ah?*"

"Da," I said. "Good. Big tits. Nice ass."

"Beeg tits, nice ahs," he said, his hands up like scales, weighing the desirability of each description. He jerked the steering wheel over, slid into a space three hairs bigger than the Land Cruiser, turned, and gave me a big thumbs-up. "Beeg tits, nice ahs, I love America!"

The New World Café was the Capital's one reliably American hangout. Inside was a woman I recognized as Genghis Ron's secretary and thus my archenemy, a pair of guys in bran-colored suits who worked for the Capital's American Chamber of Commerce, and the smiling Korean triplet waitresses, daughters of the New World's owner. I paid for my customary four cups of coffee, my cold hamburger, and my roll that was as hard as a piece of concrete and sat down at a table alone.

I was bored. Days in the Capital were the worst. Usually I holed up in my bedroom, listening to *Let It Bleed* on my headphones, sometimes putting in an appearance at my job to make a few ceremonial bribes. I don't know if I had one friend in the Capital I'd ever seen while the sun was up. I was puzzling over the unbelievability of that when he walked in.

Of all the young American Do-Gooders I'd seen dragging their crushed aspirations behind them, gushing stale idealism the way a slashed tire gushes air, I don't know why I felt any urge to pal around with this one. Maybe it was my hangover, or my remorse at how I'd treated my mother. Maybe it was guilt. How many times had I seen the Professional Expats dick around with the Do-Gooders in the New World? One of those poor glassy-eyed kids would stumble in, looking to hear some English after going without for weeks, deluding himself into thinking that just because we all knew which sport the San Diego Chargers played we were also friends when we saw each other. The Expats would ignore them, then start talking extra-loud about their satellite televisions. Even though I thought the Do-Gooders were crazy, this stuff made me wince. The only people who deserved that kind of torment were making country music.

The Do-Gooder stood in the café's doorway, his fists furiously clenching and unclenching. His blond hair was butched on the sides and slightly longer and tousled on top (a haircut he'd probably given himself). In his hand was a cache of official-seeming white papers. He hopefully scanned from table to table—looking for someone I (and he) already knew was not there—and by the time his gaze fell on me his face was crushed and long and pliant.

He ambled over to the cash register, ordered in bad Russian (all three triplets spoke English), and turned to face the café holding a paper cup of Fanta and a grease-spotted boat of warmed-up french fries. That was when I stood, pulled out a chair from my flimsy plastic table, and invited him to join me.

He considered me with a sort of queasy smile, then looked over his own shoulder, like a complete nimrod, to make sure I was talking to him. "Yeah," I said. *"You."*

He shook his head in a surprised, flattered way,

marched up to me, set his order on the table, and extended his hand. "Hey, thanks," he said. "I'm Ryan."

"Howyadoin'?" I said, briefly shaking with him. His grip was lackluster, his hand moist. "Alec."

"Yeah," he said. "I know. The ambassador's son, right?"

"That's right." We looked at each other and smiled. We sat down. After a few moments Ryan quietly ate a french fry and picked at a silvery psoriatic scab on his forehead. I finished what was left of my third cup of coffee.

"So," I said, after a minute of silence, "who were you looking for?"

Ryan looked at me with a french fry peeking out his mouth, his chin swarmed with small red stars of acne. "Huh?"

"When you came in here. You were looking for someone."

"Oh. Yeah." He briefly looked into his lap. "Someone was going to meet me here. She said if she wasn't around when I got here she wasn't coming. I wasn't really expecting to see her." He bit the tip off a fry. "I'm leaving the country tomorrow."

"Vacation?"

"No. For good. Forever."

I didn't say anything. Ryan didn't either. Instead, he straightened the edges of what I now knew were his dismissal papers.

I looked at him. "Which organization are you with?"

He stared at the papers and didn't answer me. I asked him again. He looked up, startled, and rubbed his eyes.

"God, I'm sorry. I just . . . I can't think. CARA. I'm with CARA."

I nodded. CARA: the Central Asian Relief Agency. Missionaries were illegal anywhere in the country, and CARA was one of the first groups to figure out that since volunteers could be invited by the Capital as engineers and nurses and teachers, why not start a relief agency that sent *Christian* engineers, nurses, and teachers? So you can imagine what it was like for the locals: You sent your kids off to their English lesson, only to have them come back blabbing about King Solomon and John of Patmos. My dad got more official complaints about CARA than he did about any other American agency. The Capital wanted them gone.

"So you were a missionary," I said.

To his credit, he immediately fessed up. "I guess so. I mean, I tried to be. It's hard."

This I believed. Though the country surrounding the Capital was nominally Muslim, everyone—including non-Russians—drank vodka, smoked cigarettes, and engaged in a good deal of the old rumpy pumpy. "Well," I said to Ryan, "I'll give you guys credit for having gargantuan balls."

"For what?"

"For trying to convert a bunch of Muslims to Christianity when they're not even interested in being Muslims."

"Oh," he said. "Thanks." He sat there holding a half-eaten french fry, staring again at his dismissal papers. That was when I noticed the wedding ring—a simple dimmed gold band.

I looked him in the eye. "You married?"

He nodded, frowning.

"Is she here or back home?"

He cleared from his throat what sounded like a fist-sized wad of phlegm. "Home," he said, with difficulty.

"It'll be good to see her again, I bet."

He smiled a little, lifted his hand off the dismissal papers, delicately slid his ring from his finger, and dropped it into his glass of Fanta. With a soft *plunk* it struck the cup's bottom, leaving a trail of chemically reactive bubbles popping at the soda's orange surface.

I looked at the bubbles. "Your marriage could be better, I take that to mean."

He ran a hand into his hair, plowing it back from his forehead and revealing a thinning window's peak and a bright red sore at the hairline. "Yeah."

Things began clicking into place. "This person you were meeting, this 'she'—are you porking this girl?"

Some affirmative sound grunted out of him.

"And your wife found out."

He shook his head back and forth.

I leaned back in my chair, having heard about CARA's method of dealing with indiscreet adulteries, premarital dalliances, and other generally evil living: outright dismissal, no trial, no appeal. Just because I'd heard about this punishment didn't mean I believed they actually enforced it. In a weird way I was impressed. From a pragmatic standpoint, though, enforcing rules like that was no way to run an overseas operation, since eventually everyone figures out that fucking is one of the only things

138

that improves the farther you get from America. "CARA found out," I said.

Hands still clenching his hair, he nodded.

"Well, Ryan, that's a tough one."

He looked up at me with sudden dry-eyed conviction. "I'm a sinner, and a fornicator. My forgiveness lies in the hands of God."

"That's one way of looking at it."

"It's what they told me. I just left their office."

"Who told you?"

"The director of CARA. Mr. Vandewiele."

I burst out laughing. "Let me tell you something about your Mr. Vandewiele. First of all, he's a major-league drinks-his-own-aftershave drunk. Second of all, the guy's embezzled half of CARA's dough into a private stateside account." This was common knowledge around the embassy; it seemed weird everyone else wouldn't know it too. "Man," I said, shaking my head, "it's one thing for them to boot you out, but I can't believe they let that hypocritical old lizard call you a degenerate before they did it."

Ryan folded his arms and leaned back in his chair. "You think CARA's staff knows what he's doing?"

"Of course they do. The SNB"—that is, the KGB— "has their offices bugged. Our embassy gets all the transcripts hand-delivered. All in the New World Order's spirit of cooperation."

Ryan looked away.

"You don't seem very surprised."

"In the past nine months," Ryan said, "I've repeatedly

had to go to the bathroom in a hole. Horse has been a dietary staple. I've been stoned, mugged twice, and harassed by the SNB. I'd never tasted alcohol in my life before I came here, but I managed to spend an entire week drunk. I've been in three fistfights, two of them with children. I cheated on my wife twenty-seven times, nearly lost my faith in God, and in the meantime successfully managed to evangelize only ten people."

"That's not too bad. Only two less than Jesus."

"So if you tell me that Mr. Vandewiele is a drunkard and an embezzler, then no, I'm not surprised. Not anymore. I am beyond surprise as an experience or an emotion." He blinked, his eyes the veiny, cloudy red of boiled shrimp. "All I want now is to go home. That's it."

"Where's home?"

"New Jersey. That's where my wife and my divinity school are."

"What possessed you to leave New Jersey for here?"

Ryan pushed away his boat of french fries. "I have no idea." He looked at me, a fist up to his mouth. "How about you? Where are you from?"

I shrugged. "Nowhere, everywhere."

"Where'd you go to college?"

"College of Life."

He stared at me, puzzled, then nodded sharply and looked away. He chewed at his thumbnail, his right leg bouncing under the table. How he'd made it through nine months of life outside the Capital I had no idea.

I clapped him on the shoulder. "Hey, there. Cheer up. When's your flight leave?"

"Tomorrow afternoon." This said as if it were two thousand years away.

"Okay. Perfect. I've got it. Tonight we're going to a restaurant that isn't a certifiable shithole. Then we're going to a dance club to watch Russian breasts bounce up and down. And then it's back to the Hotel Ta-Ta for your first good night's sleep in months. How does that sound?"

His eyes widened. "The Ta-Ta?"

I showed him the palms of my hands. "Relax. It's my treat. All of it."

"I don't know . . ." he said, with a new, almost street-wise wariness about him.

"Yes, you do know. Where are you staying now?"

"The Hotel Chorsu."

"The Chorsu!"

"Look, Alec," he said, standing, "thanks for the offer, but I have to go and—"

I grabbed his rayon sleeve and eased him back down. "Listen to me. You've lived like a goddamn animal for— what, *months*, right? Don't you deserve one night, one measly night of splendor? How much does CARA pay you guys, anyway?"

He told me.

"No, seriously," I said. When he didn't answer, I realized he wasn't joking. I continued, delicately. "I think you *need* this, Ryan."

He looked away, shaking his head. Suddenly he coughed out a disbelieving laugh. He turned to me. "Why are you doing this?"

"Because I'm a hell of a good guy. Why do you think?"

He looked around the café. "It all sounds nice. It does. I just . . . I don't think I could repay you."

"Nonsense. I've got more money than ten popes."

"I . . . I don't know." With a finger he fished his wedding ring from the cup of Fanta, wiped it off on his shirt, and pocketed it. He bit his lip, the pink draining to white where tooth met skin, and then he nodded hard to himself. "All right. What the hey. Let's do it. Except for that club part. I don't know if that's my speed, exactly. Despite everything I just told you, Alec, I'm still, you know"—his nose scrunched up—"a *Christian.*"

I smiled and stirred the contents of a sugar packet into my last cup of coffee. "Golly, Ryan. You don't say?"

—◦—

We walked out of the café to see a violent struggle going on in the backseat of the Land Cruiser, but I realized it was only Sergei fooling around with the Tatar girl. My heart sank a little, seeing something my father often said once again proved true: every beautiful girl in the Capital was either for sale or willing to negotiate. Sergei was always dropping my name to get girls. It would be easy to get judgmental about Sergei, but the guy had had an awful life. His family was exiled to the Capital after Stalin killed his father, his grandfather, and three of his uncles. Now he was just a measly percentage point in the Capital's shrinking Russian population. He could have used my name to get in the pants of every girl from the Capital to Islamabad, for all I cared.

"That's my truck there," I told Ryan as we approached the Toyota. "I'll break this up and we can split."

Before I could, though, the Tatar girl fell out of the Toyota with her shirt on inside out and backwards, wiping her chin. I figured for Ryan this would trigger a rectitudinous meltdown, so I turned to him and started to say something. Ryan just stared at the girl as she reached around and fixed her twisted bra strap. When she finished, he looked over at me and said, "Let's go."

I soon realized that Having Fun was a pretty dainty concept. It certainly wasn't withstanding all the weight I was piling on it for Ryan's sake. (There isn't even a word for *fun* in Russian; how's *that* for revealing?) As much as I tried, he wouldn't cheer up. In his hotel room, Sergei and I were laughing and kicking roach corpses at each other while Ryan packed up his gear. In a lull we looked over to see Ryan sitting cross-legged on the floor, his face plunged into his hands. Sergei hoisted Ryan up, took him into his arms the way only a Russian male can, removed a flask of vodka from his breast pocket, and tenderly proffered it. The stuff Sergei drank belonged in a medicine cabinet, but Ryan tipped the flask and dumped it down his gullet. He nodded in thanks, took a bleary-eyed steadying sidestep, and returned it to Sergei, who peered into its shadowy opening in astonishment. I took advantage of the moment to cry out, "To the Ta-Ta!"

Now he and Sergei were drinking in the Ta-Ta's restaurant as if they'd fought Napoleon together. We'd had our four-course dinner, half a dozen appetizers, drinks, everything. Inviting Sergei might have been a mistake. The guy had the alcoholic-intake capacity of ten men. Surprisingly, Ryan wasn't faring too badly against him, getting down one drink to Sergei's every three. The restaurant was large and spare, its decor severe, its "atmospheric" lighting like that of a fish tank. The tab we'd started at the beginning of the evening was creeping into territory so astronomical that waiters and cooks and waitresses were all huddling around the restaurant's bar, peering at the tab and then, hands to breasts, looking over at us.

I was drinking Black Label. Ryan and Sergei were chasing tequila shots with bad Turkish beer. Between Sergei's long Russian toasts I listened to Ryan dissect his troubled heart. He was young—my age—and had been married for two years. It seemed that Ryan's wife ("a good woman," he kept saying, "a good woman") tended to interact with his pork sword as though it were made of poison ivy. The wife's father was CARA's stateside accountant, which made Vandewiele's improprieties even more vexing. I asked why he was here alone, and he explained they were prepared to evangelize together until his wife failed her physical. "She's a little overweight," Ryan said quietly. But he still wanted to do it, and she wanted him to do it too.

"She sounds like a wacko," I said.

Sergei took delighted, sleepy-faced note of this word. *"Vacko,"* he said, chuckling thickly.

"She's not a wacko," Ryan protested, softly shaking his head. He closed his eyes, his face dark with resignation. "You don't understand."

"Vacko," Sergei said again, nodding off.

Unbidden came Ryan's tales of Christian persecution. Thrown rocks, SNB wiretaps, outright assaults. None of it was Saint Paul on the Appian Way or anything, but scarring enough for a divinity school grad from New Jersey, I'd imagine.

Finally we arrived at the shores of his unfaithfulness. By the standards I was familiar with, the story was tame. Moist things had developed between him and another CARA volunteer named Angela, Ryan flushing as he described how their trysts had become progressively more "wicked." I pressed for details but, sadly, received none. Now he was afraid of who he'd become. He had desires now, cravings and doubts, and felt adrift on a sea of whims and decidedly un-Christian stimuli.

"Sounds like you've become a human being," I said.

A hollow smile spread on Ryan's face. "I belong to the world."

This sounded promising to me. "Now you're talking straight, Ryan. You're goddamn right you do!"

" *'Because you do not belong to the world,'* " Ryan said, " *'I have chosen you.'* "

I frowned. "What the hell was that?"

"That," Ryan said, "was Jesus talking to his disciples."

"My opinion on Jesus," I said, "is that he was probably a nice guy who wound up in the wrong place at the wrong time." I raised my hand, ordering another round.

Ryan rubbed his face and said, "Wonderful. Can I go to my room and sleep now?"

I felt frustration spread its wings in my chest. I suddenly wanted to reach across the table and slap him, grab him by his boyish hair, and remind him that, unlike some of us, he had a life to go back to. I was within moments of throwing silverware when a skullful of soothing perfume wafted into my nostrils and I felt a hand fall lightly on my shoulder.

I turned to see a tall Russian woman in a short tight black dress standing next to me. She was one of those Capital women you saw only in places like the Ta-Ta or in pricey clubs. Her wrists were ringed with onyx bracelets; her earrings were stylish black hoops, her hair was an enormous black vortex, a spray-hardened shell. "Comrade Schiavo," she said, smiling. Her lipstick was either black or a deep sooty red.

"*Zdraste,*" I said, seeing Ryan's jaw drop open like a chain-snapped portcullis. Sergei had passed out.

Her hand rose from my shoulder and fluttered around stylishly. "Oh, no, no, no, ze Russian is unnecessary," she said. She pouted. "You don't remember me, Alec?"

Had I screwed this woman? I didn't think so. If I had I would have run around spray-painting it on the sidewalks. "I—I'm not sure," I said.

"How embarrassing for me," she said, with a loud,

solitary laugh. "I am Lena, acqvaintance of your friend Trenton. Ve met at party, two months ago, I sink."

Trent was a Shark who worked for Boeing, the kind of guy you wound up doing cocaine with if you were around him for longer than five minutes. I remembered the party. At least, I remembered arriving at the party. "Oh, yeah. Trent's party."

She laughed again. "You are a terrible liar, Alec." She extended her hand. I took it and she yanked me up from my chair. "You vill make it up to me viz dance at Dutch Club."

The Dutch Club was a mobster-haunted hive across town, a place I knew Ryan didn't have a chance in. I looked over at him, eyebrows raised in apology. "Well," I said, glad to be rid of his sad-sack bullshit.

"Yeah," he said, nodding, standing up, wobbling a little. "Thanks for everything, Alec. Maybe, you know, I'll see you again sometime."

"No, no, vait, vait," Lena said, stepping between us. "Your friend"—she put a black-fingernailed hand on Ryan's acne-splotched cheek—"von't be coming to Dutch Club viz us?"

"I've got a flight tomorrow," Ryan said, swallowing.

Lena nuzzled up against him—they were the same height—and put a hand on Ryan's left hip, her fingernails raking across his blue jeans. "Alec," she said, looking over at me, "vhat is your silly friend's name?"

"Ryan," I said.

"Vhy is your friend Ryan such idiot?"

"Maybe you should ask him."

Her face moved toward his, stopping when her black lips brushed against the cracked fissures of his. "Vhy von't you come to Dutch Club, idiot? Come dance viz me. Fuck your stupid flight."

Ryan looked at me for help, his face a twitchy, nervous white orb. I said nothing.

Lena stepped away from Ryan and looped her arm through mine. We started to walk away, Lena's rump swaying so broadly it smacked me on the hip with every step. "Wait!" Ryan called. We turned. With a guilty-looking smile Ryan was behind us, dragging Sergei, one of the table's chairs upended behind them.

Underneath the Dutch Club's neon sign were the words AMERICAN DANCE CLUB in English, and even though it was probably the hippest place in the Capital, it fell a little short of this. For one thing, you don't find many Kalashnikov-toting security guards in American dance clubs, and usually the hookers don't outnumber the patrons, a mathematical goof tricky enough to send that Malthus guy home thinking. The rest of the formula—seizure-inducing lights, manufactured smoke, music so loud it felt as if something were laying eggs in your eardrum—they had down cold.

We deposited Sergei in the back of the Land Cruiser and stumbled up to the Dutch Club's entrance. I was drunker than I thought, and by this point Ryan was having trouble finishing his sentences. Already I could tell Lena and I were not going to happen, at least not tonight. I'd taken it upon myself to drive, and Lena spent the trip across town sitting in Ryan's lap, sticking her tongue down his throat and fishing her hand into his pants. Ryan fought back with a weird mixture of total surrender followed by violent rebuff. When he pushed her away Lena would laugh—throaty, loud, off-putting—and continue undeterred. The Dutch Club guard manning the velvet rope recognized me and waved us inside, past the surly line that spanned two blocks.

Once we were in, Lena got behind Ryan and shoved him out onto the dance floor the way a bully might push a kid into a school bathroom for a beating. The dance floor was not too crowded and Lena hit its scarred vinyl planks atwirl, then lapsed into some incredibly intricate serpentine rumba that had her wrapping herself around Ryan, who was obviously *way* out of his fucking league. I was tempted to get him back to the Ta-Ta but stopped myself when I saw the look on his face. He stood in the floor's precise center, grinning, clapping out of time, bobbing like a cork, while Lena vamped all around him. Soon the floor filled up with fat, tieless, Nike-wearing mafiosi and their teenage whores in sheer black stockings and fake pearls. Lena and Ryan disappeared in the tangle. He had one night left, I thought. It might as well be a good one.

I waded through the ocean of whores to the bar, ordered a drink, and struck up a conversation with a fey young girl named Tanya. The next thing I knew I was getting blown in a corner of the Dutch Club's women's bathroom while a bevy of women crowded around the mirror to reapply their makeup. It wasn't very good—Tanya kept nicking me with her teeth—and the fact that I wasn't yet sure if she was a whore or not made it a little hard to concentrate. Paying for sex is just about the biggest turnoff I can imagine, other than shitting in a hole. Tanya must have sensed my distance because she wrapped her lips around me even tighter and squeezed my balls with her free hand about twice as hard as was necessary. Two people were fucking in one of the stalls next to us. Outside the bathroom, techno-bass pounded in Kong-summoning booms. I closed my eyes and imagined Lena blowing me instead. It seemed unbelievable that I wouldn't remember her, especially if she was at Trent's party. I'd screwed some mutty German girl at Trent's party, hadn't I? I suddenly remembered freebasing, together with Trent, a thimbleful of coke that filled my head with icy confidence and then stumbling into a bedroom with her. And wasn't it a little fucking odd—this I thought with sudden, startling clarity—that Lena was a friend of Trent's, since everyone pretty much knew that Trent was as gay as a picnic basket?

My eyes opened. I glanced down to see a puzzled Tanya shaking my nontumescent dick. She looked up at me with a shy wet-lipped smile and said, in heartbreaking English, "Me no good, Meester Alec?" *Oh, Ryan*, I thought, *oh, buddy*, zipped up, gave Tanya ten dollars American, and strode out to find him.

It didn't take long. They were still on the dance floor, grinding and making out like two teenagers, Ryan's hands clutching the globes of Lena's ass. There was no other way to do it: I walked up to them, peeled them apart, and then pushed Lena away hard on her breastless chest. She tumbled back and sat down on the floor, looking up at me open-mouthed and muss-headed, her lipstick smeared all over her face and one of her strappy black shoes hanging from her big toe. "You stay the fuck away!" I shouted, and grabbed Ryan by the arm.

I got across the dance floor before he figured out what was happening. When we reached the edge he turned to go back, his face a twist of drunken spite. "What the hell, Alec!" he said, trying to pull away. "Just what the hell?" His arms were flailing, his eyes half closed.

"Come on," I said, "we're leaving. Fun's over."

"I want that girl." He looked back at Lena. She was still sitting on the floor, watching us, lights flashing across her black dress.

"No, you don't," I said, giving him a good hard yank on his arm. "Come on, Christian. Time to go."

A low blow, maybe, but it worked. He stopped struggling and looked back at her briefly. When he turned to me, some shiny sense of belated recognition was sparkling in his eyes. "Why don't I want her, Alec?"

"Let's go, Ryan." Even though he'd figured it out, I couldn't bear telling him.

Now he grabbed me, both his hands digging into my white button-down shirt. "Why *don't* I, Alec?"

"Look," I said, as one Russian pop song gave way to another—indistinguishable—Russian pop song, "we've got to go. All right?"

What happened next is kind of hard to describe.

151

Something caught my attention—I don't remember what—and at the same time Ryan wildly swung his arm back to wrestle it free from mine. He'd caught me off guard and so his arm went flying without any resistance. The song had ended, the floor was clearing, and walking right behind Ryan was a squat, crooked-nosed gangster. Ryan's elbow caught him in the face, breaking his sunglasses and, from the look of it, doing some serious damage to the guy's eye. He swore, bent over, cupping his eye, and when he looked up at us it was as if his eyeball had been injected with a syringeful of blood. He started saying something in Russian—too quickly for me to understand—and then a flat-topped goon in a squarish suit had Ryan in a headlock. Ryan didn't fight—didn't do anything—he only kind of hung there, like a Puritan in the stocks. It was left to me to punch the guy, and when I hit him, I guess the force was with me. I mean, I killed him, though I didn't find that out until a lot later. All I remember is this satisfying feeling of something hard going *splat* under my knuckle—this must have been his nose—and he let go of Ryan as if I'd said the magic words.

That we made it out of the club was a miracle. That we made it to the Toyota was a miracle. And that no one shot us as we were peeling out was a miracle. But I realized the miracle quiver was empty when minutes later I looked in the rearview mirror and saw two Mercedes-Benzes on our tail and rapidly closing the distance. There was a cellular phone in the glove box, which I had to scream at Ryan twelve times to get for me—he was gone, he'd lost it—but finally he did. He said, *"Here! Here! Take it!"* and covered his face with his hands. That was the last thing I heard the poor kid say: *"Here! Here! Take it!"* Pretty shitty last words, I think. Anyway, I called the embassy switchboard, shouted into the phone what was happening, where we were, that I was driving as fast as I could. Sergei woke up in the backseat and said something to me. I heard a pop, and then another. Suddenly I couldn't steer worth shit; they'd shot out the Land Cruiser's tires. The next thing I remember is picking glass from my hair. I'd flipped the Toyota, apparently, trying to turn too fast on too few tires, and we went tumbling through the front window of an *apteka*, a pharmacy.

I didn't have a scratch on me, not a single fucking mark. And I hadn't even been wearing my seat belt. The Toyota was upside down, all its windows shattered. A lot of the broken glass from the pharmacy's big windows had splashed inside the Toyota, too, so my only problem was all the glass in my hair. Relieved, happy, I started picking the shit out, piece by piece. Then I looked over at Ryan. There's some debate whether or not he was dead by then. All I can tell you is that if he wasn't dead he was going to be soon: A massive, nasty shard of glass had pierced his throat, severing his right carotid artery. His eyes were open and there wasn't much blood yet, so it was very tempting to start talking to him because he didn't look that bad. I mean, there was a huge piece of glass sticking out of his throat, but not anything too bad. I tried to get out of the car but couldn't, so I sat there next to Ryan, looking into his eyes, while somewhere behind us tires bit into cement and car doors slammed.

They pulled Ryan out first. The instant they moved his body, blood started squirting. Sergei and I were next. Sergei's nose looked like a smashed ketchup bottle, and he was bawling—too drunk, I think, to understand what was happening. They dragged us into the middle of the deserted street and pushed us to our knees. I'll never get over how empty the streets were. It wasn't even that late yet—eleven, maybe midnight. I saw Ryan's body, face down, next to an open manhole, the guy he'd hit with his elbow standing with one foot on Ryan's neck. He kicked Ryan in the ribs a few times—his hand still cupped over his eye—then pulled out a small handgun and shot Ryan twice in the head. Again, there was no blood, and Ryan's body didn't even seem to register that it had been shot. It was like the guy had blanks in his gun. Maybe I've seen too many movies, but it was strange. They pushed his body into the manhole. I don't remember hearing a splash.

They shot Sergei next. This happened so quickly I'm sad we never got to say anything to each other. One moment we're kneeling there side by side, the next a pop explodes next to my ear and Sergei flops face-first onto the pavement. Why they waited to do me, I don't know, but the guy who shot Ryan and the guy who shot Sergei had an impromptu conference while the third and fourth guy held my arms behind my back. I've been told it was because they knew who I was, but I doubt it. Why, then, would they have executed Sergei? You don't fuck with the embassy, and every gangster knew it.

Anyway, it doesn't matter. Genghis Ron and a fleet of embassy security vehicles pulled up half a minute later.

The mobsters gave up without a fight, probably since they knew they had the receipt on every judge in the Capital. Back at the embassy, Genghis Ron read me the riot act. The next day I was on a plane back to Washington, where I spent a week eating room service and sleeping with a medium-attractive congressional page I picked up on the Mall and not answering the phone in my hotel room, which rang every seventeen seconds. Back in the Capital, my father was a dervish of spin, working the hush-up gears like a seasoned apparatchik. Not that it mattered. A BBC reporter (a young lady, it retrospectively occurs to me, whose visiting sister I probably should not have slept with and never called again) broke the story and—well, there's no need for me to go on. You know the rest.

I do feel awful that my dad lost his job. None of it was *his* fault. I feel awful for Ryan's family too, which is a big part of the reason my lawyer wanted me to tell *my* side of the story—to demonstrate that their wrongful-death suit is, in his words, "misguided." It's my hope that I've done so.

As for the man I killed, there might be some trouble. I doubt anything much will come of it—I *was* the ambassador's son, after all—but I'm being arraigned, if you can believe that, in the Capital next month. As slight as the chance may be, my lawyer says, I have to prepare myself for the fact that I might yet see the interior of a Capital prison cell. *Prepare* myself, the guy says. Gee, if you put it that way, I suppose I can *prepare* myself. Why I hired an American lawyer I have no idea. I'm told, though, that some of the cells have flush toilets. I'll have to look into that.

God Lives in
St. Petersburg

God, in time, takes everything from everyone. Timothy Silverstone believed that those whose love for God was a vast, borderless frontier were expected to surrender everything to Him, gladly and without question, and that those who did so would live to see everything and more returned to them. After college he had shed America like a husk and journeyed to the far side of the planet, all to spread God's word. Now he was coming apart. Anyone with love for God knows that when you give up everything for Him, He has no choice but to destroy you. God destroyed Moses; destroyed the heart of Abraham by revealing the deep, lunatic fathom at which his faith ran; took everything from Job, saw it did not destroy him, and then returned it, which did. Timothy reconciled God's need to destroy with God's opulent love by deciding that, when He destroyed you, it was done out of the truest love, the deepest, most divine respect. God could not allow perfection; it was simply too close to Him. His love for the sad, the fallen, and the sinful was an easy uncomplicated love, but those who lived along the argent brink of perfection had to be watched and tested and tried.

Timothy Silverstone was a missionary, though on the orders of his organization, the Central Asian Relief Agency, he was not allowed to admit this. Instead, when asked (which he was, often and by everyone), he was to say he was an English teacher. This was to be the pry he would use to widen the sorrowful, light-starved breach that, according to CARA, lay flush across the heart of every last person in the world, especially those Central Asians who had been cocooned within the suffocating atheism of Soviet theology. "The gears of history have turned," the opening pages of Timothy's CARA handbook read. "The hearts of 120 million people have been pushed from night into day, and all of them are calling out for the love of Jesus Christ."

As his students cheated on their exams, Timothy drifted through the empty canals between their desks. His classroom was as plain as a monk's sleeping quarters; its wood floors groaned with each of his steps. Since he had begun to come apart, he had stopped caring whether his students cheated. He had accepted that they did not understand what cheating was and never would, for just as there is no Russian word that connotes the full meaning of *privacy,* there is no unambiguously pejorative word for *cheat.* Timothy had also stopped trying to teach them about Jesus because, to his shock, they already knew of a thoroughly discredited man who in Russian was called Khristos.

Timothy's attempts to create in their minds the person he knew as Jesus did nothing but trigger nervous, uncomfortable laughter he simply could not bear to hear. Timothy could teach them about Jesus and His works and His love, but Khristos grayed and tired his heart. He felt nothing for this impostor, not even outrage. Lately, in order to keep from coming apart, he had decided to try to teach his students English instead.

"Meester Timothy," cried Rustam, an Uzbek boy with a long thin face. His trembling arm was held up, his mouth a lipless dash.

"Yes, Rustam, what is it?" he answered in Russian. Skull-clutching hours of memorizing vocabulary words was another broadsword Timothy used to beat back coming apart. He was proud of his progress with the language because it was so difficult. This was counterbalanced by his Russian acquaintances, who asked him why his Russian was not better, seeing that it was so simple.

After Timothy spoke, Rustam went slack with disappointment. Nine months ago, moments after Timothy had first stepped into this classroom, Rustam had approached him and demanded (actually using the verb *demand*) that Timothy address him in nothing but English. Since then his memorized command of English had deepened, and he had become by spans and cubits Timothy's best student. Timothy complied, asking Rustam, "What is it?" again, in English.

"It is Susanna," Rustam said, jerking his head toward the small blond girl who shared his desk.

Most of Timothy's students were black-haired, sloe-eyed Uzbeks like Rustam—the ethnic Russians able to do so had fled Central Asia as the first statues of Lenin toppled—and Susanna's blond, round-eyed presence in the room was both a vague ethnic reassurance and, somehow, deeply startling.

Rustam looked back at Timothy. "She is looking at my test and bringing me distraction. Meester Timothy, this girl cheats on me." Rustam, Timothy knew, had branded onto his brain this concept of cheating and viewed his classmates with an ire typical of the freshly enlightened.

Susanna's glossy eyes were fixed upon the scarred wooden slab of her desktop. Timothy stared at this girl he did not know what to do with, who had become all the children he did not know what to do with. She was thirteen, fourteen, and sat there, pink and startled, while Rustam spoke his determined English. Susanna's hair held a buttery yellow glow in the long plinths of sunlight shining in through the windows; her small smooth hands grabbed at each other in her lap. All around her, little heads bowed above the clean white rectangles on their desks, the classroom filled with the soft scratching of pencils.

Timothy took a breath, looking back to Rustam, unable to concentrate on what he was saying because Timothy could not keep from looking up at the row of pictures along the back wall of his classroom, where Ernest Hemingway, John Reed, Paul Robeson, and Jack London stared out at him from plain wooden frames. An identical suite of portraits—the Soviet ideal of good Americans—was found in every English classroom from here to Tbilisi. Timothy knew that none of these men had found peace with God. He had wanted to give that peace to these children. When he had come to Central Asia, he felt peace with God as a great glowing cylinder inside of him, but the cylinder had grown dim. He could barely even feel God anymore, though he could still hear Him, floating and distant, broadcasting a surflike static. There was a message woven into this dense noise, Timothy was sure, but no matter how hard he tried he couldn't decipher it. He looked again at Rustam, who had stopped talking now and was waiting for Timothy's answer. Every student in the classroom had looked up from their tests, pinioning Timothy with their small impassive eyes.

"Susanna's fine, Rustam," Timothy said finally, turning to erase the nothing on his blackboard. "She's . . . okay. It's okay."

Rustam's forehead creased darkly, but he nodded and returned to his test. Timothy knew that, to Rustam, the world and his place in it would not properly compute if Americans were not always right, always good, always funny and smart and rich and beautiful. Never mind that Timothy had the mashed nose of a Roman pugilist and a pimply face; never mind that Timothy's baggy, runneled clothing had not been washed for months; never mind that once, after Rustam had asked about the precise function of *do* in the sentence "I do not like to swim," Timothy had stood at the head of the class for close to two minutes and silently fingered his chalk. Meester Timothy was right, even when he was wrong, because he came from America. The other students went back to their exams. Timothy imagined he could hear the wet click of their eyes moving from test to test, neighbor to neighbor, soaking up one another's answers.

Susanna, though, did not stir. Timothy walked over to her and placed his hand on her back. She was as warm to his touch as a radiator through a blanket, and she looked up at him with starved and searching panic in her eyes. Timothy smiled at her, uselessly. She swallowed, picked up her pencil, and, as if helpless not to, looked over at

Rustam's test, a fierce indentation between her yellow eyebrows. Rustam sat there, writing, pushing out through his nose hot gusts of air, until finally he whirled around in his seat and hissed something at Susanna in his native language, which he knew she did not understand. Again, Susanna froze. Rustam pulled her pencil from her hands—she did not resist—snapped it in half, and threw the pieces in her face. From somewhere in Susanna's throat came a half-swallowed sound of grief, and she burst into tears.

Suddenly Timothy was standing there, dazed, rubbing his hand. He recalled something mentally blindsiding him, some sort of brain flash, and thus could not yet understand why his palm was buzzing. Nor did he understand why every student had heads bowed even lower to their tests, why the sound of scratching pencils seemed suddenly, horribly frenzied and loud. But when Rustam—who merely sat in his chair looking up at Timothy, his long face devoid of expression—lifted his hand to his left cheek, Timothy noticed it reddening, tightening, his eye squashing shut, his skin lashing itself to his cheekbone. And Timothy Silverstone heard the sound of God recede even more, retreat back even farther, while Susanna, between sobs, gulped for breath.

Naturally, Sasha was waiting for Timothy in the doorway of the teahouse across the street from the Registan, a suite of three madrasas whose sparkling minarets rose up into a haze of metallic blue-gray smog. Today was especially bad, a poison petroleum mist lurking along the streets and sidewalks and curbs. And then there was the heat, a belligerent heat. Moving through it felt like breathing hot tea.

Timothy walked past the tall bullet-shaped teahouse doorway, Sasha falling in alongside him. They did not talk—they rarely talked—even though the walk to Timothy's apartment in the Third Microregion took longer than twenty minutes. Sasha was Russian, tall and slender with hair the color of new mud. Each of Sasha's ears was as large and ornate as a tankard handle, and his eyes were as blue as the dark margin of atmosphere where the sky became outer space. He walked next to Timothy with a lanky, boneless grace, in blue jeans and imitation-leather cowboy boots that clomped emptily on the sidewalk. Sasha's mother was a history teacher from Timothy's school.

When his drab building came into sight, Timothy felt the headachy swell of God's static rushing into his head. It was pure sound, shapeless and impalpable, and as always he sensed some egg of sense or insight held deep within it. Then it was gone, silent, and in that moment Timothy could feel his spirit split from his flesh. *For I know,* Timothy thought, these words of Paul's to the Romans so bright in the glare of his memory they seemed almost indistinct from his own thoughts, *that nothing good dwells within me, that is, in my flesh. I can will what is right, but I cannot do it.*

As they climbed the stairs to Timothy's fifth-floor

apartment, Sasha reached underneath Timothy's crotch and cupped him. He squeezed and laughed, and Timothy felt a wet heat spread through him, animate him, flow to the hard, stony lump growing in his pants. Sasha squeezed again, absurdly tender. As Timothy fished for the keys to his apartment door, Sasha walked up close behind him, breathing on Timothy's neck, his clothes smelling—as everyone's clothes here did—as though they had been cured in sweat.

They stumbled inside. Sasha closed the door as Timothy's hands shot to his belt, which he tore off like a rip cord. He'd lost so much weight, his pants dropped with a sad puff around his feet. Sasha shook his head at this—he complained, sometimes, that Timothy was getting too skinny—and stepped out of his own pants. Into his palm Sasha spit a foamy coin of drool, stepped toward Timothy, and grabbed his penis. He pulled it toward him sexlessly, as if it were a grapple he was making sure was secure. Sasha laughed again and threw himself over the arm of Timothy's plush red sofa. Sasha reached back and with medical indelicacy pulled himself apart. He looked over his shoulder at Timothy, waiting.

The actual penetration was always beyond the bend of Timothy's recollection. As if some part of himself refused to acknowledge it. One moment Sasha was hurling himself over the couch's arm, the next Timothy was inside him. *I can will what is right, but I cannot do it.* It began slowly, Sasha breathing through his mouth, Timothy pushing farther into him, eyes smashed shut. What he felt was not desire, not lust; it was worse than lust. It was worse than what drove a soulless animal. It was some hot tongue of fire inside Timothy that he could not douse— not by satisfying it, not by ignoring it. Sometimes it was barely more than a flicker, and then Timothy could live with it, nullify it as his weakness, as his flaw. But without warning, in whatever dark, smoldering interior shrine, the flame would grow and flash outward, melting Timothy's core—the part of himself he believed good and stead-fast—into soft, pliable sin.

Timothy's body shook as if withstanding invisible blows, and Sasha began to moan with a carefree sinless joy Timothy could only despise, pity, and envy. It was always, oddly, this time, when perched on the edge of exploding into Sasha, that Timothy's mind turned, again, with noble and dislocated grace, to Paul. *Do not be deceived!* he wrote. *Fornicators, idolaters, adulterers, male prostitutes, sodomites . . . none of these will inherit the kingdom of God. And this is what some of you used to be. But you were washed, you were sanctified, you were justified in the name of Lord Jesus Christ and in the Spirit of our God.* It was a passage Timothy could only read and reflect upon, praying for the strength he knew he did not have. He prayed to be washed, to be sanctified in the name of Jesus, but now he had come apart and God was far from him. His light had been eclipsed, and in the cold darkness that followed, he wondered if his greatest sin was not that he was pushing himself into nonvaginal warmth but that his worship was now for man and not man's maker. But such taxonomies were of little value. God's world was one of cruel mathematics, of right and wrong. It was a world that those who had let God fall from their hearts condemned as repressive and awash in dogma—an accurate but vacant condemnation, Timothy knew, since God did not anywhere claim that His world was otherwise.

A roiling spasm began in Timothy's groin and burst throughout the rest of his body, and in that ecstatic flooded moment nothing was wrong, nothing, with anyone, and he emptied himself into Sasha without guilt, only with appreciation and happiness and bliss. But then it was over, and he had to pull himself from the boy and wonder, once again, if what he had done had ruined him forever, if he had driven himself so deeply into darkness that the darkness had become both affliction and reward. Quickly Timothy wiped himself with one of the throw pillows from his couch and sat on the floor, sick and dizzy with shame. Sasha, still bent over the couch, looked back at Timothy, smirking, a cloudy satiation frosting his eyes. *"Shto?"* he asked Timothy. *What?*

Timothy could not—could never—answer him.

⌁

The next morning Timothy entered his classroom to find Susanna seated at her desk. Class was not for another twenty minutes, and Susanna was a student whose arrival, on most days, could be counted on to explore the temporal condition between late and absent. Timothy was about to wish her a surprised "Good morning" when he realized that she was not alone.

A woman sat perched on the edge of his chair, wagging her finger and admonishing Susanna in juicy, top-heavy Russian. Her accent was unknown to Timothy, filled with dropped *G*s and a strange diphthongal imprecision. Whole sentence fragments arced past him like softballs. Susanna merely sat there, her hands on her desktop in a small bundle. Timothy turned to leave but the woman looked over to see him caught in mid-pirouette in the doorway. She leaped up from his chair, a startled gasp rushing out of her.

They looked at each other, the woman breathing, her meaty shoulders bobbing up and down, her mouth pulled into a rictal grin. *"Zdravstvuite,"* she said stiffly.

"Zdravstvuite," Timothy said, stepping back into the room. He tried to smile, and the woman returned the attempt with a melancholy but respectful nod. She was like a lot of women Timothy saw here: bull-necked, jowled, of indeterminate age, as sexless as an oval. Atop her head was a lumpen yellow-white mass of hair spray and bobby pins, and her lips looked as sticky and red as the picnic tables Timothy remembered painting, with his Christian youth group, in the parks of Green Bay, Wisconsin.

"Timothy Silverstone," she said. *Teemosee Seelver-stun.* Her hands met below her breasts and locked.

"Yes," Timothy said, glancing at Susanna. She wore a bright bubble gum–colored dress he had not seen before, some frilly ribboned thing. As if aware of Timothy's eyes on her, Susanna bowed over in her chair even more, a path of spinal knobs surfacing along her back.

"I am Irina Dupkova," the woman said. "Susanna told

me what happened yesterday—how you reacted to her . . . problem." Her joined hands lifted to her chin in gentle imploration. "I have come to ask you: This is true, yes?"

Her accent delayed the words from falling into their proper translated slots. When they did, a mental dead bolt unlocked, opening a door somewhere inside Timothy and allowing the memory of Rustam's eye swelling shut to come tumbling out. A fist of guilt clenched in his belly. *He had struck a child.* He had hit a boy as hard as he could, and there was no place he could hide this from himself, as he hid what he did with Sasha. Timothy felt faint and humidified, his face pinkening. "Yes, Irina Dupkova," he said, "it is. And I want to tell you I'm sorry. I . . . I—" He searched for words, some delicate, spiraled idiom to communicative his remorse. He could think of nothing, entire vocabularies lifting away from him like startled birds. "I'm sorry. What happened made me . . . very unhappy."

She shot Timothy a strange look, eyes squinched, her red lips kissed out in perplexion. "You do not understand me," she said. This was not a question. Timothy glanced over at Susanna, who had not moved, perhaps not even breathed. When he looked back to Irina Dupkova she was smiling at him, her mouthful of gold teeth holding no gleam, no sparkle, only the metallic dullness of a handful of old pennies. She shook her head, clapping once in delight. "Oh, your Russian, Mister Timothy, I think it is not so good. You do not *vladeyete* Russian very well, yes?"

"*Vladeyete,*" Timothy said. It was a word he was sure he knew. "*Vladeyete,*" he said again, casting mental nets. The word lay beyond his reach somewhere.

Irina Dupkova exhaled in mystification, then looked around the room. "You do not know this word," she said in a hard tone, one that nudged the question mark off the end of the sentence.

"Possess," Susanna said, before Timothy could lie. Both Timothy and Irina Dupkova looked over at her. Her back was still to them, but Timothy could see that she was consulting her CARA-supplied Russian-English dictionary. *"Vladeyete,"* she said again, her finger thrust onto the page. "Possess."

Timothy blinked. *"Da,"* he said. *"Vladeyete.* Possess." For the benefit of Irina Dupkova, he smacked himself on the forehead with the butt of his palm.

"Possess," Irina Dupkova said, as if it had been equally obvious to her. She paused, her face regaining its bluntness. "Well, nevertheless, I have come here this morning to thank you."

Timothy made a vague sound of dissent. "There is no need to thank me, Irina Dupkova."

"You have made my daughter feel very good, Timothy. Protected. Special. You understand, yes?"

"Your daughter is a fine girl," Timothy said. "A fine student."

With that Irina Dupkova's face darkened, and she stepped closer to him, putting her square back to the doorway. "These filthy people think they can spit on Russians now, you know. They think independence has made them a nation. They are animals, barbarians." Her eyes were small and bright with anger.

Timothy Silverstone looked at his scuffed classroom

floor. There was activity in the hallway—shuffling feet, children's voices—and Timothy looked at his watch. His first class, Susanna's class, began in ten minutes. He moved to the door and closed it.

Irina Dupkova responded to this by intensifying her tone, her hands moving in little emphatic circles. "You understand, Timothy, that Russians did not come here willingly, yes? I am here because my father was exiled after the Great Patriotic War Against Fascism. Like Solzhenitsyn, and his careless letters. A dark time, but this is where my family has made its home. You understand; we have no other place but this. But things are very bad for us now." She flung her arm toward the windows and looked outside, her jaw set. "There is no future for Russians here, I think. No future. None."

"I understand, Irina Dupkova," Timothy said, "and I am sorry, but you must excuse me, I have my morning lessons now, and I—"

She seized Timothy's wrist, the ball of her thumb pressing harshly between his radius and ulna. "And this little hooligan Uzbek thinks he can touch my Susanna. You understand that they are animals, Timothy, yes? *Animals*. Susanna," Irina Dupkova said, her dark eyes not leaving Timothy's, "come here now, please. Come let Mister Timothy see you."

In one smooth movement Susanna rose from her desk and turned to them. Her hair was pulled back into a taut blond ponytail and lay tightly against her skull, as fine and grained as sandalwood. She walked over to them in small, noiseless steps, and Timothy, because of his shame for striking Rustam before her eyes, could not bear to look at her face. Instead he studied her shoes—black and shiny, like little hoofs—and the sapling legs that lay beneath the wonder of her white leggings. Irina Dupkova hooked Susanna close to her and kissed the top of her yellow head. Susanna looked up at Timothy, but he could not hold the girl's gaze. He went back to the huge face of her mother, a battlefield of a face, white as paraffin.

"My daughter," Irina Dupkova said, nose tilting downward into the loose wires of Susanna's hair.

"Yes," Timothy said.

Irina Dupkova looked over at him, smiling, eyebrows aloft. "She is very beautiful, yes?"

"She is a very pretty girl," Timothy agreed.

Irina Dupkova bowed in what Timothy took to be grateful acknowledgment. "My daughter likes you very much," she said, looking down. "You understand this. You are her favorite teacher. My daughter loves English."

"Yes," Timothy said. At some point Irina Dupkova had, unnervingly, begun to address him in the second-person familiar. Timothy flinched as a knock on the door sounded throughout the classroom, followed by a peal of girlish giggling.

"My daughter loves America," Irina Dupkova said, ignoring the knock, her voice soft and insistent.

"Yes," Timothy said, looking back at her.

"I have no husband."

Timothy willed the response from his face. "I'm very sorry to hear that."

"He was killed in Afghanistan."

173

"I'm very sorry to hear that."

"I live alone with my daughter, Timothy, in this nation in which Russians have no future."

Lord, please, Timothy thought, *make her stop.* "Irina Dupkova," Timothy said softly, "there is nothing I can do about any of this. I am going home in three months. I cannot—I am not able to help you in that way."

"I have not come here for that," she said. "Not for me. Again you do not understand me." Irina Dupkova's eyes closed with the faint, amused resignation of one who had been failed her whole life. "I have come here for Susanna. I want you to have her. I want you to take her back to America."

Struck dumb had always been a homely, opaque expression to Timothy, but he understood, at that moment, the deepest implications of its meaning. He had nothing to say, nothing, and the silence seemed hysterical.

She stepped closer. "I want you to take my daughter, Timothy. To America. As your wife. I will give her to you."

Timothy stared her in the face, still too surprised for emotion. "Your daughter, Irina Dupkova," he said, "is too young for such a thing. *Much* too young." He made the mistake of looking down at Susanna. There was something in the girl Timothy had always mistaken for a cow-like dullness, but he could see now, in her pale eyes, savage determination. He suddenly understood that Susanna's instigation lay behind Irina Dupkova's offer.

"She is fourteen," Irina Dupkova said, moving her hand, over and over again, along the polished sheen of

Susanna's hair. "She will be fifteen in four months. This is not so young, I think."

"She is too young," Timothy said, with a fresh anger. Again he looked down at Susanna. She had not removed her eyes from his.

"She will do for you whatever you ask, Timothy," Irina Dupkova was saying. "Whatever you ask. You understand."

Timothy nodded distantly, a nod that both understood but did not understand. In Susanna's expression of inert and perpetual unfeeling, he could see that what Irina Dupkova said was right: She *would* do whatever he asked of her. And Timothy Silverstone felt the glisten of desire at this thought, felt the bright glint of a lechery buried deep in the shale of his mind. *My God*, he thought. *I will not do this.* He was startled to realize he had no idea how old Sasha was. Could that be? He was tall, and his scrotum dangled between his legs with the heft of postadolescence, but he was also lightly and delicately haired, and had never, as far as Timothy could tell, shaved or needed to shave. Sasha could have been twenty-two, three years younger than Timothy; he could have been sixteen. Timothy shook the idea from his head.

"I have a brother," Irina Dupkova was saying, "who can arrange for papers that will make Susanna older. Old enough for you, in your nation. It has already been discussed. Do you understand?"

"Irina Dupkova," Timothy said, stepping backward, both hands thrust up, palms on display, "I cannot marry your daughter."

Irina Dupkova nearly smiled. "You say you cannot. You do not say you do not want to."

"Irina Dupkova, *I cannot do this for you.*"

Irina Dupkova sighed, chin lifting, head tilting backward. "I know why you are here. You understand. I know why you have come. You have come to give us your Christ. But he is useless." Something flexed behind her Slavic face plate, her features suddenly sharpening. *"This* would help us. *This* would save."

Timothy spun around, swung open his classroom door, poked his head into the hallway, and scattered the knot of chattering children there with a hiss. He turned back toward Irina Dupkova, pulling the door shut behind him with a bang. They both stared at him, Irina Dupkova's arm holding Susanna close to her thick and formless body. "You understand, Timothy," she began, "how difficult it is for us to leave this nation. They do not allow it. And so you can escape, or you can marry." She looked down at herself. "Look at me. This is what Susanna will become if she remains here. Old and ugly, a ruin." In Irina Dupkova's face was a desperation so needy and exposed Timothy could find quick solace only in God, and he tried to imagine the soul within Susanna, the soul being held out for him to take away from here, to sanctify and to save. That was God's law, His imperative: *Go therefore and make disciples of all nations.* Then God's distant broadcast filled his mind, and with two fingers placed stethescopically to his forehead Timothy turned away from Irina Dupkova and Susanna and listened so hard a dull red ache spread behind his eyes. The sound disappeared.

"Well," Irina Dupkova said with a sigh, after it had become clear that Timothy was not going to speak, "you must begin your lesson now." Susanna stepped away from her mother and like a ghost drifted over to her desk. Irina Dupkova walked past Timothy and stopped at his classroom door. "You will think about it," she said, turning to him, her face in profile, her enormous back draped with a tattered white shawl. "You will consider it." Timothy said nothing and she nodded, turned back to the door, and opened it.

Students streamed into the room on both sides of Irina Dupkova like water coming to a delta. Their flow hemmed her in, and Irina Dupkova's angry hands fluttered and slapped at the black-haired heads rushing past her. Only Rustam stepped aside to let her out, which was why he was the last student into the room. As Rustam closed the door after Irina Dupkova, Timothy quickly spun to his blackboard and stared at the piece of chalk in his hand. He thought of what to write. He thought of writing something from Paul, something sagacious and unproblematic like *We who are strong ought to put up with the failings of the weak.* He felt Rustam standing behind him, but Timothy could not turn around. He wrote the date on the board, then watched chalk dust drift down into the long sulcated tray at the board's base.

"Meester Timothy?" Rustam said finally, his artificial American accent tuned to a tone of high contrition.

Timothy turned. A bruise like a red-brown crescent lay along the ridge of Rustam's cheekbone, the skin there taut and shiny. It was barely noticeable, really. It was nothing. It looked like the kind of thing any child was liable to get, anywhere, doing anything. Rustam was smiling at him, a bead of wet light fixed in each eye. "Good morning, Rustam," Timothy said.

Rustam reached into his book bag and then deposited into Timothy's hand something Timothy remembered telling his class about months and months ago, back before he had come apart—something that, in America, he had said, students brought their favorite teachers. It got quite a laugh from these students, who knew of a different standard of extravagance needed to sway one's teachers. Timothy stared at the object in his hand: an apple. Rustam had given him an apple. "For you," Rustam said softly. He turned and sat down.

Timothy looked up at his classroom to see five rows of smiles. Meester Timothy will be wonderful and American again, these smiles said. Meester Timothy will not hit us, not like our teachers hit us. Meester Timothy will always be good.

Woolen gray clouds floated above the Registan's minarets, the backlight of a high hidden sun outlining them in gold. Some glow leaked through, filling the sky with hazy beams of diffracted light. Timothy walked home, head down, into the small breeze coming out of the foothills to the east. It was the first day in weeks that the temperature had dipped below 38°C, the first day in which walking two blocks did not soak his body in sweat.

Sasha stood in the tall doorway of the teahouse, holding a bottle of orange Fanta in one hand and a cigarette in the other. Around his waist Sasha had knotted the arms of Timothy's gray-and-garnet St. Thomas Seminary sweatshirt (Timothy didn't recall allowing Sasha to borrow it), the rest trailing down behind him in a square maroon cape. He slouched in the doorway, one shoulder up against the frame, his eyes filled with an alert, dancing slyness. He let the half-smoked cigarette drop from his fingers, and it hit the teahouse floor in a burst of sparks and gray ash. He was grinding it out with his cowboy-boot tip when Timothy's eyes pounced upon his. *"Nyet,"* Timothy said, still walking, feeling on his face a light spatter of rain. *"Ne sevodnya, Sasha."* Not today, Sasha. Timothy eddied through the molded white plastic chairs and tables of an empty outdoor café, reached the end of the block, and glanced behind him.

Sasha stood there, his arms laced tight across his chest, his face a twist of sour incomprehension. Behind him, a herd of Pakistani tourists was rushing toward the Registan to snap pictures before the rain began.

Timothy turned at the block's corner even though he did not need to. In the sky a murmur of thunder heralded the arrival of a darker bank of clouds. Timothy looked up. A raindrop exploded on his eye.

—

Timothy sat behind his work desk in his bedroom, a room so small and diorama-like it seemed frustrated with itself, before the single window that looked out on the over-planned Soviet chaos of the Third Microregion: flat roofs, gouged roads that wended industriously but went nowhere, a domino of faceless apartment buildings just like his own. The night was made impenetrable by thick curtains of rain, and lightning split the sky with electrified blue fissures. It was the first time in months it had rained long enough to create the conditions Timothy associated with rain: puddles on the streets, overflowing gutters, mist-cooled air. The letter he had started had sputtered out halfway into its first sentence, though a wet de facto period had formed after the last word he had written (*here*) from having left his felt-tip pen pressed against the paper too long. He had been trying to write about Susanna, about what had happened today. The letter was not intended for anyone in particular, and a broken chain of words lay scattered throughout his mind. Timothy knew that if only he could pick them up and put them in their proper order, God's message might at last become clear to him. Perhaps, he thought, his letter was to God.

Knuckles against his door. He turned away from his notebook and wrenched around in his chair, knowing it was Sasha from the lightness of the three knocks, illicit knocks that seemed composed equally of warning and temptation. Timothy snapped shut his notebook, pinning his letter between its flimsy boards, and winged it onto his bed. As he walked across his living room, desire came charging up in him like a stampede of fetlocked horses; just before his hand gripped the doorknob he felt himself through his Green Bay Packers sweatpants. A sleepy,

squishy hardness there. He opened the door. Standing in
the mildewy darkness of his hallway was not Sasha but
Susanna, her small nose wrinkled and her soaked hair a
tangle of spirals molded to her head. "I have come," she
said, "to ask if you have had enough time to consider."

Timothy could only stare down at her. It occurred to
him that he had managed to let another day go by without
eating. He closed his eyes. "Susanna, you must go home.
Right now."

She nodded, then stepped past him into his open,
empty living room. Surprise rooted Timothy to the floor-
boards. "Susanna—" he said, half reaching for her.

After slipping by she twirled once in the room's center,
her eyes hard and appraising. This was a living room that
seemed to invite a museum's velvet rope and small engraved
plaque: SOVIET LIFE, CIRCA 1955. There was nothing but the
red sofa, a tall black lamp that stood beside nothing, and a
worn red rug that did not occupy half the floor. Susanna
seemed satisfied, though, and with both hands she grabbed
a thick bundle of her hair and twisted it, water pattering
onto the floor. "We can fuck," she said in English, not looking at him, still twisting the water from her hair. She pronounced it *Ve con fock*. She took off her jacket and draped it
over the couch. It was a cheap white plastic jacket, something Timothy saw hanging in the bazaars by the thousand.
Beneath it she was still wearing the bubble gum dress, aflut-
ter with useless ribbonry. Her face was wet and cold, her
skin bloodless in the relentless wattage of the lightbulb
glowing naked above her. She was shivering.

Timothy heard no divine static to assist him with

Susanna's words, only the awful silent vacuum in which the laws of the world were cast and acted upon.

"We can fuck," Susanna said again.

"Stop it," Timothy said.

"We can," she said in Russian. "I will do this for you and we will go to America."

"No," Timothy said, closing his eyes.

She took a small step back and looked at the floor. "You do not want to do this with me?"

Timothy opened his eyes and stared at the lamp that stood next to nothing. He thought that if he stared at it long enough, Susanna might disappear.

"I have done this before with men."

"You have," Timothy said—it was a statement—his throat feeling dry and paved.

She shrugged. "Sometimes." She looked away. "I know what you think. You think I am bad."

"I am very sad for you, Susanna, but I don't think that."

"You will tell me this is wrong."

Now both of Timothy's hands were on his face, and he pushed them against his cheeks and eyes as if he were applying a compress. "All of us do wrong, Susanna. All of us are bad. In the eyes of God," he said with listless conviction, "we are all sinners."

A knowing sound tumbled out of Susanna. "My mother told me you would tell me these things, because you believe in Khristos." She said nothing for a moment. "Will you tell me about this man?"

Timothy split two of his fingers apart and peered at her. "Would you like me to?"

She nodded, scratching at the back of her hand, her fingernails leaving a cross-hatching of chalky white lines. "It is very interesting to me," Susanna said, "this story. That one man can die and save the whole world. My mother told me not to believe it. She told me this was something only an American would believe."

"That's not true, Susanna. Many Russians also believe."

"God lives for Russians only in St. Petersburg. God does not live here. He has abandoned us."

"God lives everywhere. God never abandons you."

"My mother told me you would say that too." From her tone, he knew she had no allegiance to her mother. She could leave this place so easily. If not with him, she would wait for someone else. She shook her head at him. "You have not thought about marrying me at all."

"Susanna, it would be impossible. I have a family in America, friends, my church . . . they would see you, and they would know. You are not old enough to trick anyone with papers."

"Then we will live somewhere else until I can." She looked around, her wet hair whipping back and forth. "Where is your bed? We will fuck there."

"Susanna—"

"Let me show you what a good wife I can be." With a shoddy fabric hiss, her dress lifted over her head and she was naked. For all her fearlessness, Susanna could no longer meet Timothy's eye. She hugged herself, each hand gripping an elbow, her xylophonic rib cage heaving, the concave swoop of her stomach breathing in and out like that of a panicked, wounded animal. She was smooth and hairless but for the blond puff at the junction of her tiny legs. She was a thin, shivering fourteen-year-old girl standing naked in the middle of Timothy's living room. Lightning flashed outside—a stroboscope of white light— the room's single bright lightbulb buzzing briefly, going dark, and glowing back to strength.

His bedroom was not dark enough to keep him from seeing, with awful clarity, Susanna's face tighten with pain as he floated above her. Nothing could ease the mistaken feeling of the small tight shape of her body against his. After it was over, he knew the part of himself he had lost with Sasha was not salvaged and never would be. *I can will what is right, but I cannot do it.* He was longing for God to return to him when His faraway stirrings opened Timothy's eyes. Susanna lay beside him, in fragile, uneasy sleep. He was drawn from bed, pulled toward the window. The beaded glass was cool against his palms. While Timothy waited—God felt very close now—he imagined himself with Susanna, freed from the world and the tragedy of its limitations, stepping with her soul into the house of the True and Everlasting God, a mansion filled with rooms and rooms of a great and motionless light. Even when Susanna began to cry, Timothy could not turn around, afraid of missing what God would unveil for him, while outside, beyond the window, it began to rain again.

Animals in
Our Lives

The English," Franklin says, ostensibly to Elizabeth but mostly to himself. He twists the key and shifts into first, her Saturn's engine whirring. "Maybe it's all the fog and boarding school. Makes their brains soggy." He backs out of their spot in the parking lot of Frodo's, a popular Hobbit-themed pizza joint. It was the third time he had eaten at Frodo's, and its lode of wonderment only deepened. He thinks of the braid-headed waitresses wearing poofy aprons and forbidding black blouses. The dark Middle Earth decor. The signed copy of *The Fellowship of the Ring* stored within a small glass coffin near the entrance. The antiquarian's certificate of authentication that hangs above it, like an edict. The silence, neither hostile nor familiar, in which they picked at their oblong mushroom-and-cheese.

Elizabeth looks over at him as he muscles into Grand River Avenue's Sunday traffic. Her tennisy white T-shirt is soiled with a colon of tomato sauce along its V-neck. He's only now noticed and hopes she will not. Quickly he looks away. One never quite knows when the end begins. Such a strange intuitive lapse for brains so attuned to the flutter of beginnings, their nauseating spiral of joy and terror. Somehow, the beginning of the end molts recognition's casing, a phantom countdown lacking even the condolence of a synonym. After she falls asleep tonight, he will remove this shirt from the hamper, rub liquid detergent into the tiny orange stains, and let it soak overnight in the stoppered bathroom sink. He will not tell her. He will rise early, and by dawn the shirt will find itself back in the hamper. The sink will be discreetly drained. Kindness, once as uncomplicated as respiration, has a sick new venturesome quality. Anything they do for each other now is fuel for yet another misunderstanding.

"The English," she echoes blankly.

The rinse of daylight on the windshield is blinding. He jerks back and forth in his seat. "Not *all* of them. Churchill. Orwell. Nice dry brains."

She simply shakes her head, hands lifting from her smooshed thighs. A mystified entreaty to elaborate.

"Tolkien," he says. That she doesn't know what he's talking about sticks him through the heart. She would have, he thinks, once. His tone sharpens. "*The Hobbit.* Frodo's. Where you just bought us lunch."

Elizabeth gazes out her window. "Tolkien was Scottish, I thought." They are passing the zoned commercial clutter of a small midwestern university town. She is a medical student here, in the closing weeks of her second year, widely held to be the most punishing. Sometimes, late at night, he allows this to console him. She stares at the bagelries, the record and bike stores, the bars so close to one another he suspects they are in hidden, felonious league. On his side of the street is the northern flank of the university, endless greenery plunked with long flat structures terraced with rococo Modernism, gloomy campus-Gothic firetraps, stark administrative fortresses designed from the academic-industrial-complex blueprint popular in the mid-1970s.

"Tolkien was English," he points out gently.

She shrugs. Her haircut is a day old, a perky forgery of a popular television heroine's. The way her hair sweeps huggingly down her cheeks, its planed tips curling at her clavicle, creates a vague resemblance to the Greek letter omega. Her face is sere with too much studying, stress, him. "I always thought hobbits were Scottish," she says, with growing conviction. She has never, as far as he knows, surveyed any of the material one would need to support this observation. Her certainty seems to puzzle even her. She gestures. "Like, you know . . . leprechauns."

"Leprechauns are—"

"I *know* what leprechauns are."

His mouth tamps shut, the following silence like fallout. His fingers find the steering wheel's reassuring ergonomic grooves. He remembers when she enjoyed listening to him, the look of milky wonder in her eyes as he clarified and elaborated and invented. It does not seem so long ago. Suddenly he thinks of Tolkien, of the flashlit nighttime hours he'd spent reading him as a boy. The only time one really *could* read Tolkien. Tolkien had built the bridge that had allowed Franklin to travel from *Spider-Man* to *Beowulf* to Yeats to Joyce. He'd read *The Lord of the Rings* five times, which seems impossible to him now, his shelves sagging with worthy books he knows he will never read. He thinks of Tom Bombadil. Quickbeam the Ent. Gandalf Stormcrow. For three Halloweens in a row he'd dressed as Gandalf, until his cotton-ball beard went stringy and ridiculous. That does not seem so long ago either. He is twenty-five years old. *Nothing* seems so long ago.

"Tolkien was a don at Oxford," he says, after a little

while. "One day while grading papers he wrote *hobbit* in the margin of one of them. He didn't even know why. The word just came to—"

"What the *hell* kind of a name is J. R. R. Tolkien, anyway? *Three* initials? Who uses three initials?" She fixes him with a demanding stare, her mouth dropped open.

"M. F. K. Fisher," he says.

She looks at him, blinking. "I don't know who that is. Is *he* Scottish?"

He reflects, then clears the word for takeoff: "She." A mistake. No need to point that out. He has no idea why he's said it. She is a stranger to him now, and consequently he is a stranger to himself. He cannot decide if he is a kind, decent person who sometimes behaves terribly or a terrible person given to outbreaks of decency.

On her face: *You are such an ass.* She looks away, pushes hair from her temple, and settles back into the bucket seat.

They are on the highway now, headed toward Trapper's Cove Trail, an isolated apartment complex inhabited by what university housing refers to as "older students," a euphemism he knows is meant to be heartening. Two months ago he'd abandoned his job as an English teacher in Kyrgyzstan to come back here. To "work it out." He'd pulled up to Trapper's Cove Trail in a mostly empty U-Haul to find Elizabeth sitting on the curb, eating peanut-butter-and-chocolate-chip sandwiches. Her eyes blurred with tears as he leaped from the truck and embraced her. They'd smiled at each other, each time they'd passed on the stairs to her walk-up, lugging the dead storage of his old college life into her unchanged college life, box by box.

That *does* seem long ago. But he is not a student, and everything in this place reminds him of it.

A billboard floats past on their starboard side, too bright and cartoonish to disregard. He spies a camel, an elephant, a peacock. The camel and elephant are deeply familiar, defiant cribs from icons made famous by R. J. Reynolds and *Dumbo*. The peacock, having seized the foreground, shouts in a large white word balloon: COME SEE US AT POTTER'S PARK ZOO! NEXT EXIT! It makes weird sense to him that, of this bestiary, a peacock should serve as spokesanimal.

"Zoo," he says quietly. He has no idea if she's seen the billboard, if she will know what he's talking about. Read my mind, he thinks. Reconnect. Tell me what I'm asking you, because I no longer know.

"Oh, Franklin," she says, rubbing her eyes. "Anything. Anything but this."

"Lock the doors," she says getting out of the car, slipping the knot of sleeves at her midriff and punching her way into a lawn-green sweatshirt. It is emblazoned with her College of Human Medicine's logo, a quasi-federal seal wreathed high-mindedly with Latin. As her hairdo passes through the sweatshirt's cinched neck it suffers the devastating physics of static electricity. She looks at him, nervous and pie-eyed, attempting to smile. The sweatshirt hangs dented and formless from her shoulders' unsettlingly visible knobs. Since he's moved back they have dropped so much weight they seem in anorexic competition.

"Locked," he announces, using the fat remote control tethered to her key chain to fire the bolts into place. Her eyes roll instantly skyward as he double-checks the driver-side door the old-fashioned way, with his hand. He knows that Elizabeth has always believed the remote control to be technology's most benevolent gratuity. Her air conditioner has a remote control, as does her microwave. Franklin's faith in the purely tactile is a philosophical divergence they once thought charming, an enduring non-argument stoked only as an excuse to kiss and make up. He tries to ignore her double-nostriled sigh as he moves around the car to check on the passenger-side door.

They wend through a parking lot of minivans and station wagons, their shoulders docking in small, accidental bumps. Franklin chatters hopelessly, noting blacktop splatterings of mustard and ketchup that indicate likely sites of savage parent-child struggle. She looks at him in an amused, disbelieving way, then chuckles and shakes her head. Heartened, he begins to devise long, inscrutably reasoned police reports based on the sunbaked condiments' arc and angle. She shushes him suddenly, her eyes rimmed with wet light, then throws her arms around his shoulders and crushes her face against his breastbone, as though this is the Franklin she wants, *this* one, right here. And please don't change if I let go.

They pull apart, shaken, and reach the long willowy esplanade leading to Potter's Park's ticket booth. It is a bright, zephyr-bathed day. Pink and lilac flamingos stand motionless in the shoal of an adjacent pond. Peacocks and Canada geese roam freely along the sidewalk's grass borderland, close enough to startle away with a foot stomp. He has a mindless phobia of Canada geese: the reptilian atavism of their physiology, their mysterious ability to hiss, the tiny razors cunningly hidden within their beaks, their sharp and grotesquely purple tongues. Suddenly, his heart nose-dives: one goose, satanically privy to his fear, is prancing toward him. Suddenly he is awash in sweat, charging down the path with panicked composure. Somehow Elizabeth catches him and takes his hand. He doubles over, temples thrumming with blood, her palm moving in clockwise solace in the drenched small of his back. Her smell is a synthesis of tumble-dried clothes and baby powder, and he has a child's sudden faith that nothing will ever happen to him as long as she's here.

At the booth an older man with a lean arrowy face trades Franklin's money for tickets. The man smiles at them in the poignant, not quite envious way of one who has accepted his aloneness. He proffers a single map, an assumption of their indivisibility. In the aftermath of this gesture, Elizabeth looks on the brink of tears, the air above filled with the faint roar of the nearby airport's arrivals and departures. They push through the turnstile and find themselves on the gazebo overlooking Potter's Park Zoo. Across its sun-dappled plaza float small groups of three and four and five, families all. No one here is alone, yet he is unable to link wives with husbands, children with parents. Everyone either knows everyone else or is pretending to, reticence burned off in the sunshine. He knows Elizabeth is looking at him. Put her in any proximity to children and she is helpless but to midwife their own child's physiognomy in her mind. He cannot bear to look over at her. What was once a reverie is now bloodless skepticism.

Potter's Park's designers have single-mindedly eschewed cages, bars, grates, anything that suggests an overt mandate to detain rather than preserve. Four identical brick buildings with tinted glass doors angle around the zoo's centerpiece, an exposed moated rock pile draped with half a dozen California sea lions. Elizabeth is drawn toward them, down the gazebo's bleached concrete stairs, cooing. Franklin follows, transfixed by how the sunlight ignites the sea lions' fur to a bright rust, how the water slickens their coats with a petroleum sheen. They are absurdly pleasing animals, their flippers as huge as tennis rackets, their leglessness somehow mistaken, whiskers spraying from their smooth, tiny skulls.

As he joins her at the tank's polished silver rail she reads aloud from a nearby plaque.

> *"A male's harem may have as many as ten females. They bark to discourage other males from intruding on their territory."*

She turns to him, delighted with the fresh imprint of information she can, for once in her med-student hell, treasure as completely useless.

"Barking," he says. "Maybe I should have thought of that."

She takes a moment to process before her eyes cloud over and her face screws up in disbelief. "Jesus Christ," she spits, executing a turn of military precision and marching off.

As he lets her go he fills with mechanical calm. What can he tell her, this late in the game? His bouquets have been tendered, tossed back in his face, reassembled and tossed back again . . . he has nothing left with which to console her. Her beeline terminates at the nearest building, whose glass door she yanks open. She hesitates before vanishing behind its tint, frustrated that the door's slow journey shut confounds her desire to slam it. He turns back to the sea lions' tank, water slopping dreamily over its raised edge. A small, sleek black shape swims ecstatic laps, in the thrall of discovering that a circle's joy is never having to turn a corner.

~

She had broken up with him by letter—what his fellow aid workers had called a "long-distance rupture." He had wandered the hilly green streets of Bishkek with the letter stuffed in his back pocket, hoping its contents might change if he read it in a different light, beneath trees, next to a statue, at night, across town. She had offered no explanation other than "this" being "too hard." He could not write back. He did not know how. He did not know what "this" referred to. He knew only her, and him. A few weeks later his letters to her were returned, ribboned together, with a short, graceful note. He wrote back this time. For months he heard nothing. Then, one night, across twelve time zones, she called. Her testimony came forth all at once, any of its bitter serrates smoothened by rehearsal. Aaron, the man she now explained she had left him for, was gone, though it was no fresh wound; it had happened weeks ago. It seemed Aaron was something of a big-game hunter, and after he'd stared long enough into the eyes of his latest mounted trophy, the itch of the stalk sent him reaching for his pith helmet. She spared Aaron any villainy. He was a vain, childish man whose pathogens she had freely allowed to infect her.

"It was a mistake," she'd blurted, so suddenly he knew she had only now determined this. Her voice was small and echoey, easy to misunderstand. Franklin said nothing, not knowing if this moment were the harbinger of new happiness or further pain. She mistook his silence for a calculation of which he was not capable. "I'm *sorry,*" she said, gulping. "Franklin, I'm so sorry."

He could not discuss it. He hung up hollow, a scarecrow. Four days later he called her back. "I'm on the other side of the world. I don't know what you want me to do."

Her tone ossified. "*I* don't know what I want you to do."

He would say it, then. If they rebuilt and disaster ensued, he would be the negligent architect. "I could come back. We could start all over again."

"We could," she said, her voice cloaked in something gray and wistful. "We could."

"Everything will be different."

He heard, somehow, through his primitive receiver, the sound of a forlorn smile. *"All changed, changed utterly."*

He'd been stopped cold. Solitude had made her unrecognizable, florid. Then it came. The words were not hers. This was borrowed sadness—from a poem, of all things:

"Easter 1916." Yeats. Heartbreak's laureate. *What is it but nightfall? No, no, not night but death; was it a needless death after all?* Franklin felt vaguely ashamed. It had never occurred to him to flee into the arms of poetry. Cautiously he asked, "Have you been reading Yeats, Elizabeth?"

"Yeah," she said, as her tone simulcast, *And why wouldn't I be?* But they both knew why. Only one reason. To remember that well-read boy to whom she'd given her heart.

When he finally walks over to the building he sees ANIMALS IN OUR LIVES neoclassically chiseled in concrete above its double-swing doors. What such a promise might entail he is not sure. The lobby is lit with low, teakish light. Elizabeth is across the room, her back to him, standing before a window with the determined head tilt of someone teasing sense from an obscure painting. When he reaches her he sees what dwells behind the window: a pigeon. Its head is a beaked gray thumb. Its wings and tail feathers are splotched with white, as though it had slalomed through the pickets of a freshly painted fence. Its environs, Franklin realizes, are a precisely rendered tarpaper rooftop. Painted on its three walls is skyscraper iconography roughly congruent to that of New York City. The pigeon's tiny black eyes seem to demand some explanation from him.

"A pigeon," he says.

She shoots him a dark, simmering glance. " 'Animals in Our Lives.' It's a motif. Live with it."

He absorbs this strafe and sidesteps to the next window without comment. Inside is a small rain-forest simulacrum, something called a red jungle fowl standing in insulated silence. Its otherwise dun-colored breast and wings are streaked with a runny palette of green, orange, yellow. A huge tripartite red growth sits atop its head, made of tough plasticky-seeming material that is difficult to accept as skin. Its eyes blink once a second within sockets of pebbled flesh. Franklin reads its lengthy biography and learns that all chickens descend from the red jungle fowl. He is looking at nothing less than poultry's Eve.

The windows keep coming: the taveta golden weaver, the green plover, the flying squirrel. (One truism of animal nomenclature: Any creature prefixed by "flying" in fact does no such thing.) Elizabeth is unmoved until she genuflects at a bank of smallish thigh-level windows. Encased within are guinea pigs, black gerbils, piebald mice, quivering piles of hairless infant hamsters. Suddenly she is purling, clucking her tongue, shaking her head, a weird analog of motherhood. He tries to join in, snickering as he reads aloud one of the rodents' identification plates: " 'The common hamster.' As opposed to the extraordinary hamster."

She doesn't even look at him. "As opposed to the dwarf hamster right next to it."

He steps back from her. With sick precision he feels his internal armature give way. Legs first, then arms. His chest is last, collapsing upon itself with a sad, nauseating plash. Nothing works. An ache flowers behind his eyes. "Elizabeth—" he begins.

"I know," she says, nodding, her eyes mashed shut. "I know. I'm sorry."

Together they wander to the building's remaining wing. He takes her hand, she squeezing back so tightly the vestigial remnant of webbing between his fingers pulls tight. The spherical room they enter is lit more starkly than the lobby. Astounded children gambol from window to window, leaving their mouths' hot smears on the glass. Elizabeth stops at a window while Franklin, lost in his first sustained thought in days, keeps going. Her hand opens all too willingly, but he holds on and reels himself back to her. He can't recall what he was just thinking about. Something about nostalgia: nostalgia being the loss of forward motion. Stupid thoughts. Useless. He stares at her lopsided reflection in the glass. Her face is white and puffy and lovely. Her lips are full and biconvex and devastating. It has been days since they've kissed in anything other than ritual.

She stares past herself at two poison-dart frogs, their world another tiny, slapdash tropical ecosystem. A pitiful waterfall squirts from an aperture hidden in a pack of smooth rocks. He wonders if any of these creatures have the faintest idea of what's happened to them. If successful captivity is primarily a matter of fooling the captive. These frogs are toylike and beautiful, living gems, glistening in their deadly marinade. One frog—an impossibly fluorescent green with perfect black spots—leaps from rock to rock and back again. The other, the color of an oxidized bronze statue, peers up at them, pulsing intelligently.

Elizabeth sets the tips of her three longest fingers to the window. "They're beautiful."

"You're beautiful," he says.

She sighs, her forehead meeting the glass with a sad thud. She looks over at him, her longing so raw and naked that he swallows. "Oh, my love—" She stops, eyes bulging. Words that have not vibrated her vocal cords in weeks. They stare at each other as though a beast believed long extinct has poked its head up through fronds and vanished before either of them thought to document it. At that moment two loutish boys old enough to resent muscle them from their marks. They pound on the glass, elbowing each other and laughing, the frogs leaping around in a kind of post-traumatic-stress frenzy, fruitlessly attempting to hide. Instinct suddenly seems to Franklin like a painfully elaborate hoax.

Elizabeth leads him past several tanks of fish and stops at the room's final window. For two minutes they stare without speaking into a branch-crowded space the size of a computer screen, the rumored home of a New Guinea walking stick. A dent forms between Elizabeth's tweezed eyebrows. "Well . . . where the hell is it?"

He shrugs. "Maybe this is a part of the Animals *Not* in Our Lives exhibit."

They give up. Outside, the sun hits their constricted pupils like a penlight. Their hands fly up to their foreheads in protective salute. She juts her chin across the plaza. "How about some monkeys?"

Sounds of glass-blunted simian distress greet them as they push open the doors. He allows Elizabeth to forge ahead as he stops to survey humanity's evolutionary growth chart, a bit of self-congratulation customary to every monkey house. He tracks *Homo sapiens'* loss of prognathous jaw and humped back and squat cabriole legs. He notes that with each exultant step into a new taxonomy, mankind's shave grows progressively cleaner. Some wit has Magic Markered a briefcase in the hand of the family Hominidae's only extant species.

Elizabeth summons him with a giggle. "*Look* at these guys," she says, as Franklin rests his chin atop her shoulder and wraps his arms around her waist. Behind the glass a dozen cotton-topped tamarins whip through their jungle gym with impossible precision. In acrobatic lulls, small intelligent faces peer at them from beneath Warholian mops. As she watches the tamarins, he feels the furtive murk of desire. He presses himself against her rump, tastes the salt from her neck, her breasts filling the scales of his hands. She sighs, wearily indulgent, then frees herself from his grasp. "Okay there, tiger," she says, smiling.

They bypass several other spidery little hominids in favor of the hamadryas baboons. Theirs is the biggest cage they've seen yet—not a cage at all, but a barren outdoor mountainside tunneled with caverns. The net above cuts the sky into tiny blue boxes. Franklin half-reads the plaque.

> *"One of the most fearsome baboons . . .*
> *found primarily in Northern Africa and*
> *the Arabian peninsula."*

Hamadryas, he thinks, rummaging through a recondite vocabulary amassed during four semesters of ancient Greek. The word breaks pleasingly in half: Wood spirit.

The baboons emerge from their caves with dawn-of-man portent. Their faces are terrifying, their tiny eyes set too close together and fixed above wolfish snouts. They wear their huge filthy-gray coats with the sort of careless arrogance he associates with aging female movie stars. And their *asses*! Franklin tries not to look. They are hideously disproportionate, the largest posteriors he's ever seen: red, distended, inflamed, vaguely metastasized, caked with straw and fossilized shit.

Elizabeth's face crinkles. "Ick."

The last baboon to appear has silvery tufts shooting from his wizened face. That this is the alpha male there seems little doubt. Every member of his retinue turns a respectful back on him. He bares his teeth and moves with tumbling knuckle-first locomotion from one cowering female to the next, a long thin pink hard-on wagging beneath him. Franklin turns away without a word. Elizabeth follows. One can watch primates only so long before reconsidering what really makes up the celebrated 1 percent variance in man-ape DNA. Nucleotides, the opposable thumb, or something far fainter? A genealogy of manners, perhaps. Wearing napkins. Asking if this seat is taken.

Elizabeth consults their map. They decide to skip the snake house and camel ride in favor of Discovery Trail. The umbilical breezeway leading to it is filled with games whose primary purpose appears to be the humiliation of the contestant. Hash marks dare them to attempt a standing jump farther than the wallaby's. Measurements ask them to compare their wingspan to the bald eagle's. A twenty-yard-dash track, complete with a digital stopwatch, invites them to race an imaginary emu. They walk slowly, wanting to belly up to each challenge as though, in failing, they will once again appreciate humanity's cerebral consolation prize.

Discovery Trail begins its winding path in an ingeniously landscaped grove, an oasis of stillness and pollen-soaked quiet. The ground is mulched with huge sodden wood chips. Everywhere they turn they are met with explosions of elephant grass and artfully sheared shrubbery and tropical flowers, botanical exotica, once separated by continents, drinking from the same root system. Several finger-shaped ponds hem them in, make shunting the trail an impossibility. Elizabeth shrieks as a butterfly, the largest, hairiest, most malevolent butterfly he's ever seen, flutters near her face. Franklin bats it away, its weight slapping against his palm with an unsettling, velvety density. She embraces him, laughing, and, for that moment, he knows his darkly wrought love for her is irreversible, embered and glowing, hot as the day it was hammered.

She leads him happily to the trail's proper starting point, a steep tunnel-gouged strip of turf infested with prairie dogs. They are wild-eyed ravenous little monsters, scuttling in and out of their holes' crumbly passageways, chattering and whistling to one another. Some animals, he thinks, seem not to mind so much. Nothing would ever hurt them here. Captivity's sole bonus.

He looks over at her. She is smiling, the sun a pale gloss on her face. "Did you love Aaron?" Why he says this now he doesn't know. It is a question he's never asked her before, for dread of her answer. Either of them.

She turns to him with a look of pinch-eyed betrayal

that is replaced instantly with the recognition that she owes him an answer. She looks away. "I don't know. I thought I did." She empties her lungs with a ponderous sigh, her hair aglow in smooth lemony light. "Yeah. I did."

They step onto the planks of Discovery Trail's one bridge, a wooden fairy-tale construction, curved and whimsical. He glances over the rail to see a flotilla of dark, snake-headed turtles floating beneath them. When he turns back to her she is chewing dents into her lip.

"Why did you ask me that?"

His mind fills with cue cards. To know. To know why you left me. To know why I came back. To know the capacity of your heart. To know if this is our last day together. To know if it was a needless death after all. His hands find their way into pockets made roomy by a month of steady weight loss. He shrugs, the tacked-up shreds of his insides unfurling like banners.

At the other side of the bridge, Discovery Trail becomes a zoo without cages or pens, the realm of animals whose escape risk is low. An Australian goose, tall, violet, and dapper-looking, waddles alongside Elizabeth with the pride of a freedman. Peacocks made fat by castaway popcorn trail behind them, pecking hopefully at their footprints. They stop at a thin rope fence. Twenty yards away, beyond a ditch he knows must be deeper and wider than it appears, wallabies and emus wander together with the unease of unfamiliar party guests. The wallabies do not walk as much as skulk, wearing faces of sloe-eyed, mischievous kangaroos. The emus are flightless heaps of black feather above sallow, implausibly muscular legs. Their kneecaps are like small stunted heads. He remembers reading, somewhere, that emus are feared for their rib-breaking kicks. Or is it ostriches? He can't recall. He used to know so much. And he thinks, not for the first time, of the job he'd left behind.

After college he was a model of unemployability, his single skill, his sole grace, an ability to read books well. He'd sent out résumés like doves in search of dry land. None returned. Then he saw a campus poster for English-teaching positions in the former Soviet Union. Qualifications, helpfully, were not needed. Within weeks he was interviewed, and within days of his interview he had accepted their offer of placement. Before leaving he proposed to Elizabeth, her acceptance filling them both with a Quaker's inner peace in the face of separation. In Kyrgyzstan, his foolhardy resolve reaped unforeseen rewards. Parents from all over Bishkek approached him to teach their children. He learned passable Russian and sparkling Kyrgyz. He hiked the lower reaches of cloud-topped mountains and rafted rivers he convinced himself no American had ever seen. He learned to grow outraged and excited by a tiny nation's parochial shock waves, rumblings that only occasionally managed to stir the world's busy oblivious remainder. When he told his school that he had to leave, that he was experiencing personal problems at home, they offered everything they could to keep him there. His own lovely apartment, rather than a small rented room. A salary additional to that which his organization paid him, money that would have made available every possible Bishkek luxury: peanut butter, a motorcycle, even, if it came to that, the women he often saw trolling the city's better restaurants and hotels. How easy it had been to spurn the empty satisfaction of the known. He knows now that all mistakes are made with such perfect confidence.

He gestures. "That emu could just hop that ditch and go bananas out here, couldn't it? Kick little kids from now to St. Patrick's Day."

She nods sagely. "Ah, yes. The savage emu." But she thinks about it, her eyes slitting. "Maybe they're tagged. Electronically."

Tagged. Technology again. Franklin is inexplicably saddened. At least with cages one knows where one stands. He does not know why, really, he hates technology, a hatred Kyrgyzstan had only hardened. Perhaps, like any other bigot, he needs hatred's reflexive, vulgar reassurance of preservation.

They continue their exploration of Discovery Trail, stopping to gaze up at a pair of red pandas snoozing in the treetops. These creatures are a curious dog-fox blend, the stopgap work of a stagnant evolution. "Cute," she says, just as one of them yawns to reveal a wicked mouthful of yellowy incisors. Franklin laughs, too hard, and Elizabeth walks ahead, leaving him there. They police opposite sides of the trail, taking in the next few stops alone. Franklin is staring with unseemly fascination at a porcupine snacking upon a twitching grasshopper when he hears Elizabeth say, "Well, *this* is depressing."

He turns. She is standing before the bald eagle exhibit, shaking her head and making soft, aghast sounds. Twenty feet ahead of her, ballasted by talons clutched around the thin trunk of a wind-cripple sapling, sits a bald

eagle. No. Not sits. Not stands, either. There is no satis-
factory verb for its nonflight state. Franklin feels an unaccountable quickening of his pulse. This is just a bird,
after all. But *bird* is wholly unable to communicate the
essence of this animal. It is as wide in the torso as he is,
invincibly silent, motionless. Its bright yellow beak ends
in a sinister down-turned spike. The eagle seems somehow aware of its national-mascot status.

Elizabeth's distress has only deepened. "God. It's
so *sad.*"

Gently Franklin turns her five degrees to the left.
"Have a look at the plaque."

> *This eagle's foot was caught in a trap set to
> catch fur bearing animals. In addition to
> its foot injury, it experienced a wing injury
> which prevents it from flying. We are car-
> ing for this eagle because it cannot live in
> the wild anymore.*

"I don't care," she says, throwing up her arms. "They
should just kill it, then. Put it out of its misery. You can't
take care of something just because it's *hurt.*" By the last
word, she is shouting with gallant conviction. A nearby
family shies away with telepathic simultaneity.

Franklin wills the anger from his voice. "You didn't
seem too torn up about that pigeon. Or those emus."

His refusal to allow her this hypocrisy summons
wide-eyed hatred. "It's *different,*" she says.

He turns back to the crippled eagle. The sky above it

seems as open and blue as a taunt. Perhaps all we owe those we love are nods when confronted with vanity, smiles in exchange for blind sanctimony. Never itemizing. Never using weakness as collateral. Why, he wonders, should love need signifiers? True love. An inexplicable qualification, a near tautology. There is, after all, no *true* hate, no *brotherly* indifference, no *puppy* lust. We engrave love with names to preserve it in the hierarchy of our memory, the most absolutist graveyard. We name it so that it might not die. His voice sinks to a pitch of détente. "Maybe it likes it here."

"What choice does it have?" she says, bitterly rhetorical.

"Come on," he says, after a moment. "One more stop." He takes her cold, limp hand, but she doesn't budge, her sandals rooted to the ground. He simply looks at her and tugs her lifeless arm. Finally she shakes her head, her face speeding from fury to composure in a heartbeat. They are living by that heartbeat, minute by minute. Nothing is promised beyond that.

He remembers, now, reading in the *Daily Journal* how Potter's Park had volunteered for the yearlong gig of babysitting an elderly Siberian tiger named Ajax while the Cincinnati Zoo remodeled. A small block of text buried behind AP bulletins from Srebrenica and Tehran. For some reason he knows that the Cincinnati Zoo saw the last passenger pigeon die under its vigil. My God: Why does he know this? A book, he recalls, read months ago. A history of zoos, one of the hundred titles quietly acidizing on the shelves of the American Chamber of Commerce's tiny Bishkek library.

Ajax has been given Potter's Park's celebrity suite.

Franklin wonders if, somewhere in the zoo's untrafficked bowels, there is a lightless cell filled with a displaced brown bear. Ajax's grounds are as rolling and wide open and dandelion splotched as an upper-middle-class lawn. A farrago of long Stonehengish slabs of rock form a shelter beneath a shady stand of trees near the back. The cat makes good use of its space, stalking imperially from one quadrant to another, telegraphing its direction changes with a head-lifting sniff of the air. Ajax's muscles, all of them, from the long plates of his flank to the tight bunches around his neck, are splendid enough to trigger pinwheels of creationist awe. His stripes are brilliantly diverse, some tapering into spearheads, others jagged like lightning bolts, others yet arabesque swirls. Age has given over Ajax's coat to an uncertain gray-edged white. Elizabeth is breathless, drilling her fingers into his hand. This is the only animal they've seen that seems to think of its captivity as temporary.

"Wow," she says simply. "*Look* at him. It's like he's biding his time or something."

Nothing alive, it occurs to him, can be truly broken. Suddenly, as though testing her, he lets go of Elizabeth's hand. Without hesitating she stuffs it under her armpit and shivers.

He stares at Ajax. His long, unkempt whiskers are filthy with curds of meat. Who trims them? It seems a question in search of a punch line: Where does a two-ton elephant sit? Ajax, he thinks. From the Greek, of course, its journey into the King's English leaving it as roughed up and unrecognizable as the name Jesus would be to a first-century Galilean. *Aias,* from *aiai:* pain that is self-inflicted. A useful distinction. A ias the solider who did not know when to stop fighting.

Elizabeth looks over at him as though she doesn't know what's just happened. As though the casket in her mind has not just been filled. "Seen enough wildlife?"

The day's heat clogs his throat. He nods.

Her smile trembles. "Let's go home?" In the final syllable is a terrible cognizance that tears her smile in two. Home. A reflex word, summoned by striking a shared joint now withered and dead. A certainty they can at last share. After an awful half-second hesitation, she squeezes his bicep and walks away.

He wonders, as he follows her, where he will go. What he will do. But he feels a supernal calm, a numbing reconfiguration of his chemistry. He falls behind, until they no longer have even the illusion of walking together. When, much later than love would have allowed, she finally turns to find him, to pick out his face from the sudden orbiting crowd, he feels latitudes away from her, his radar gone black, at an utter loss to name this loss. Her eyes find his. She smiles. *There you are. Are you coming?* As his hand lifts, he knows nothing but the solace he will take from the sad, lovely girl who comes to him, sometimes, behind his eyes, and tells him how much she loves him. And he will live, for a little while, on that imagined bit of love, until he no longer needs it, or her, or the girl whose face she wears. This girl. You.

Author's Note

These stories were written in the following order: "Aral" (1997), "The Ambassador's Son" (1997), "God Lives in St. Petersburg" (1998), "Animals in Our Lives" (1999), "Expensive Trips Nowhere" (2000), and "Death Defier" (2002). Students of Central Asia will note that many of the stories misrepresent not a few of the region's factual particulars. The United Nations has never dispatched to the Aral Sea anything like Amanda Reese's doomed troupe of scientists from "Aral," for instance. "The Ambassador's Son" and "God Lives in St. Petersburg" fiddle creatively with the geography of Tashkent and Samarkand, respectively. "Expensive Trips Nowhere" affronts as boring the Almaty of 1997 or so, not the vibrant, interesting city of today. "Death Defier" describes the uncertain situation between the Taliban and the Northern Alliance in mid-November of 2001; while it is, in some ways, reflective of what was happening during that time in northern Afghanistan, no Afghan or Tajik folk remedy I have ever heard about involves medicinal grass. (The folk remedies of which I am aware are, if anything, far weirder.) These and other distortions—while we are at it, the Potter's Park Zoo of "Animals in Our Lives" will surely disarm anyone who has visited the actual zoo in East Lansing, Michigan—are intentional.

Author's Note

The Russian in this book has been transliterated in accord with *written* rather than *spoken* Russian—with two exceptions: *"sevodnya"* (*today*) for *"segodnya"* and *"shto"* (*what*) for *"chto."* I thank Boris Fishman, Minsk's loss and our gain, for his help here.

"Expensive Trips Nowhere" draws heavily on (and in two places directly from) Ernest Hemingway's "The Short Happy Life of Francis Macomber"; Viktor's memories were helped by Svetlana Alexievich's *Zinky Boys: Soviet Voices from the Afghanistan War.* "God Lives in St. Petersburg" is indebted to the Pauline scholarship of Wayne A. Meeks. "Death Defier" was strengthened by readings of Sherwin B. Nuland's *How We Die* and Greg Marinovich and Joao Silva's *The Bang-Bang Club.*

My profound thanks to the editors who first published these stories (in many cases years after they were written and following dozens of rejections): Ted Genoways at the *Virginia Quarterly Review;* Askold Melnyczuk and Eric Grunwald at *Agni;* Betsy Sussler and Suzan Sherman at *BOMB;* Ronald Spatz at *Alaska Quarterly Review;* Lee Epstein, Eli Horowitz, and Dave Eggers at *McSweeney's;* and Calvin Liu at *Bullfight.* Thanks, finally, to Heather Schroder, Dan Frank, Jenny Minton, and Andrew Miller, for everything.

Permissions Acknowledgments

Printed in the United States
by Baker & Taylor Publisher Services